DARK FLOWERS

A NOVEL

CAYTLYN BROOKE

H2O

LIVONIA, MICHIGAN

Cover, interior, and eBook design by
Blue Harvest Creative
www.blueharvestcreative.com

Editing by Bailey Karfelt

DARK FLOWERS

Published by H2O
an imprint of BHC Press

Library of Congress Control Number:
2016954062

ISBN-13: 978-1-946006-09-7
ISBN-10: 1-946006-09-2

Visit the author at:
www.bhcpress.com

Also available in eBook

FOR DANIEL,
for always believing in every word I write.

I believe in everything
until it's disproved.

So I believe in fairies,
the myths, dragons.

It all exists, even if
it's in your mind.

Who's to say that dreams
and nightmares aren't as
real as the here and now?

~ John Lennon ~

CHAPTER

1

ELIZA GLANCED ACROSS the table at the Head Matron, who sipped her tea with a permanent scowl etched upon her face as she listened to the nun next to her. *Just another minute.*

"Just like that, gone. No one ever saw her alive again," whispered Amy, one of the older orphan girls seated farther down the table. The younger girls seated around her gasped in unison and leaned closer.

"What happened to her? Where did she go?" a young girl named Lacey asked, her green eyes shining with a mixture of curiosity and worry.

Matron Criggs sat down her tea and turned her back completely on her charges, intent on her private conversation.

Amy smiled. "She tried to run away through the swamps. In the dead of night, she broke the lock on the window and fled, straight into the bushes. They say she just started walking, running, sprinting as fast as she could away from this place. But the swamps were pitch-black and the leaves so thick that no moonlight could be seen. She kept running and running and finally, she thought she had escaped far enough away. She took another step, almost to the little town on the other side, and fell into the black water."

The girls gasped again as Eliza rolled her eyes. This version of the story of the missing orphan girl couldn't be true. She bit her tongue from pointing out the obvious flaws and instead made her move toward Matron Criggs' tea.

"But she might have made it," Lacey insisted. "She could have climbed out and made it to the town."

"True. But she didn't," Amy replied quietly. "For she forgot one very important thing...alligators."

Next to Eliza, another girl with dark brown hair clutched the edge of the table in fear, but not in response to Amy's story.

"Eliza, stop it, you're gonna get in trouble," cautioned eleven-year-old Millie.

Eliza rolled her eyes and finished pouring the ink into the head matron's tea. "Don't be such a baby," she scoffed under her breath, slipping the half-empty glass bottle back into the folds of her sleeves just as Matron Criggs turned back to her tea.

"Alligators?" one of the girls was saying. "Did they eat her?"

Amy shrugged and moved her fork through her starchy mashed potatoes. "No one knows. A few days later, a search team went out and tried to find her. They even took a few hounds. Then, after hours of searching, one of the dogs came back with something in its mouth, something pale and cold and thin."

The table was silent, each girl dreading the next words.

"The dog brought back an arm. Celia's *severed* arm," Amy hissed, looking as horrorstruck as her spellbound audience. "There were even teeth marks at the end where the gators had chomped it in half."

"No!" all the girls cried, their eyes wide with disbelief.

Eliza scoffed.

"It's true," Amy insisted. "Celia used to be my old roommate when I first got here."

Immediately arguments struck up between the girls as they discussed the details of the story. Millie turned toward the sudden swell of voices and pulled on Eliza's sleeve. "What are they talking about? Who is Celia?"

Eliza shushed Millie out of the corner of her mouth and watched with growing anticipation as Matron Criggs picked up her teacup with two hands, inhaled the sweet fragrance, and raised it to her lips.

Here we go!

Setting her teacup down, Matron Criggs licked her newly blackened teeth and frowned when she noticed Eliza staring at her. "What are you looking at? Eyes down and eat your peas," she scolded.

Snapping to attention at the Matron's voice, all the girls stopped talking and returned to their meals. Eliza inwardly groaned as the youngest orphan gathered her courage and asked, "I was wondering...is the story about Celia true, ma'am?"

"Celia?" Matron Criggs snorted. "What story? The one of how the gators took big bites out of her?"

The little girl nodded and looked down, biting her lower lip.

"It's garbage," Matron Criggs barked. "No one gets out of here unless I say so." The head nun took another sip of her tea, spreading the ink to her lips. She looked down at the girls and smiled widely, her mouth a giant black hole in the center of her wrinkled face.

As one the girls averted their eyes.

Matron Criggs sucked in a quick breath through her teeth and narrowed her eyes. "Do you think one of these girls has something else to say, Sister Emily?"

Sister Emily, one of the younger nuns and the one member of the staff that Eliza liked, looked up from her lumpy mashed potatoes and tilted her head. "Something else to say? I'm not sure what you— oh Matron! Your mouth, it's black!"

"Black?" the Matron repeated, not looking surprised. She grabbed her teacup and looked inside. "Ink in my tea," she sneered. "Clever. And who was the little brat who came up with this latest scheme?"

In an act of rare harmony, the girls remained silent, their faces betraying nothing. Matron Criggs studied each girl in turn, until her eyes at last alighted on Eliza.

Eliza stared back at the nun defiantly, a smirk tugging on the corner of her lips.

"I should have known," Matron Criggs spat. "Miss Eliza Q. I believe it's off to the box for you."

Eliza pushed back her plastic chair and stood. "And I believe you really need to see a dentist," she replied, batting her eyelashes.

The girls gasped in unison. The box was far more terrifying than the story of Celia's demise.

"Liza, stop it," Millie hissed, grabbing hold of Eliza's plaid skirt.

Matron Criggs' foul smile widened. "Make that two days in the box!" Faster than the girls could blink, the woman rounded the table and dug her sharp nails into Eliza's upper arm. "Let's be off then, shall we?"

Eliza allowed herself to be dragged from the dimly lit cafeteria and down a winding hall, until Matron Criggs stopped before a waist-high door, bouncing a set of brass keys in her hand. Finding the correct one, she sorted it out from the others and unlocked the door. The well-oiled hinge swung open, revealing only darkness.

"In you go, you little brat," the Matron ordered with obvious glee as she pushed Eliza through the opening.

The box had once been a janitor closet, but Matron Criggs had done some redecorating to make it as uncomfortable as possible for a child waiting out their punishment. It was called "the box" for a reason; it allowed no light or fresh air, and offered no reprieve for a weary offender. Eliza noted the smell of urine was particularly strong today. There was no bathroom in the box.

Gritting her teeth, Eliza ducked underneath the divider. Inside she was only able to turn around and stare straight ahead. She had been a guest to the box many times, during her stay at the orphanage, but never for two whole days. Tiny shivers ran down her spine but she refused to apologize or beg. She had known what her punishment would be when she smuggled the ink bottle out of the library and she was proud. Someone had to stand up to Matron Criggs, and if she was the only one brave enough, then so be it.

"I hope you ate enough at dinner, because that's all you'll be getting until Thursday," Matron Criggs spat. "Sweet dreams." With a clang, she slammed the door shut and total blackness enveloped Eliza.

Welcome to St. Agatha's Home for Girls, Eliza thought.

CHAPTER 2

ELIZA AWOKE WITH a start as the metal door to her black prison smashed against the outer wall. For the past two days, she had been trapped inside the box with no food, no water, no sunlight, no communication, and no hope.

The purpose of the box was sensory deprivation. Matron Criggs believed that this form of punishment was effective in curtailing deviant behavior in the girls. Eliza suspected she liked to hear them scream as the thick blackness took control.

Startled by an abrupt noise, Eliza felt a stream of hot urine run down the inside of her skirt, trickling down onto the floor she lay on. "God, get me out of here," she whispered miserably.

"Come on out, my dear," Sister Emily whispered.

Eliza perked up for a moment, surprised to hear the gentle nun's voice rather than the harsh voice of the Matron. Pushing herself off the musty back wall, Eliza crawled from her prison with weak, shaking limbs. The bright fluorescent lights lining the hallway burned her enlarged pupils and she shrank back into the box for a moment.

"There, there," Sister Emily comforted, staying a sensitive distance away. "It's all over now. Perhaps this latest visit to the box will prevent further misconduct, hmmm?"

Eliza knew Sister Emily hated the concept of the box, but the headmistress's orders were never questioned. Using the wall for support, Eliza crawled out with shaking legs. After the first three hours of confinement her legs had gone numb.

"Oh dear," Sister Emily whispered, stepping forward to catch Eliza from hitting the floor.

"Thank you," Eliza coughed. Impulsively she wrapped her arms around the nun's waist.

"Now, now, none of that, my dear," Sister Emily said gently as she untangled herself from Eliza's embrace.

Although Eliza knew the other nuns would tattle if they saw the physical contact, after two days of severe isolation, Sister Emily's rejection was too much. Tears sprang to her eyes and her arms dangled uselessly at her sides.

"Please, Miss Eliza, no tears," whispered Sister Emily. "You know the rules."

Eliza nodded.

"Now, let's get you cleaned up and ready for dinner. I'm sure you're starving."

Eliza nodded again, and with a quiet sniffle and quick swipe of her hand, all evidence of her momentary weakness was gone. She turned away from the nun, stomach growling, and went to move in the direction of the dormitories. On the first shaky step, her knees gave out.

Sister Emily reacted instantly, catching and lowering Eliza gently to the floor before walking quickly down the hall.

Eliza's cheeks burned with embarrassment when the nun returned with a wheelchair. Although she would never admit it, she was relieved to take a seat, even with her soiled skirt pressing cold and wet against her legs. She hoped Sister Emily couldn't smell her.

Sister Emily set off briskly, and even the air in the hallway was refreshing after the past forty-eight hours. Eliza closed her eyes and soaked it in. She could have used conversation, but the Matron disliked chatter almost as much as she did physical contact.

Sister Emily wheeled the chair to a stop in front of Eliza and Millie's shared room and smiled at Eliza. "If you want to go in and grab your shower supplies and a towel, I'll wait here."

Eliza nodded and carefully lowered her feet to the floor, using the nearby wall to help support the majority of her body weight. Sister Emily looked away, unable to offer her assistance. Eliza breathed out slowly and hobbled to the door, her legs weak from hours of not moving. She knew it wasn't Sister Emily's fault. If anyone saw the nun helping her, or simply holding her hand, Criggs would be informed

"I'll be right back," Eliza whispered over her shoulder as she grasped the cold handle and pushed the door open. At the sound of the door, Eliza saw Millie's dark head turn and a large smile spread across her friend's face.

"Eliza! You're back!" Millie squealed as Eliza crossed the threshold into their room. She waited for the door to click shut and gave her friend a quick hug. "What was it like in there for *two* days? You probably almost died." Though shy, Millie had a wild imagination that even the Matron had yet to break.

Eliza shrugged and collapsed onto the stiff mattress. "It was fine. It smelled really bad but I think next time I'll go for three days. It was a nice break," she lied. Even around Millie she hated being vulnerable, and found herself constantly fabricating stories and telling lies to appear tough.

The two girls could not have been more different. Millie was petite, with pale skin and blue eyes, and had come to the orphanage two months ago after her family's home burned to the ground, with her mother, father, and older brother trapped inside. Millie had been at a friend's house when it happened and was soon after brought to St. Agatha's.

From Millie's stories, Eliza knew the girl had once been adventurous, but Millie's only adventures now happened in her dreams. Eliza hoped that a nice family would adopt her soon and save her from the orphanage. The orphanage's monthly Adoption Day was next week, and Millie would be the pick of the litter in Eliza's opinion.

In comparison, Eliza was a little older, tall and blonde, had dark amber eyes, and didn't miss her family at all, because she had never had one. She had been kicked out of numerous foster homes ever since her mom threw her away. Five weeks ago her case worker had reached her last straw and brought Eliza to St. Agatha's as a last resort before juvenile hall. After only a few weeks, Eliza already held the record for the longest time in the box.

Unlike Millie, Eliza didn't harbor any dreams of being adopted. She had already tried living with families and been given away by each for not playing nice with their other children. Eliza didn't understand it, but knew from experience another family would think no different. Each night, when Millie prayed for a nice family to find her, Eliza planned her escape. Adoption was a lost cause for her; the only way to get out was to run.

As Eliza stared up at the yellowed-popcorn ceiling, she remembered what the Matron had said at dinner before her trip to the box. *No one gets out of here unless I say so.*

Yeah, maybe no one but me. Eliza smiled.

Millie wrinkled her nose, noticing the stench of old and new urine permeating the small room. "Wow, you weren't kidding, you reek!" she cried, plugging her nose.

"I know, I know," Eliza chuckled, remaining on the bed. "Sister Emily is going to take me to shower."

"Well, yeah! I think I need one too—you hugged me. Now I'm smelly!" Millie joked and rose to her feet. Eliza, knowing she couldn't keep the nun waiting any longer, slowly rolled off the mattress and landed with a clumsy thud on her feet.

"Are you okay?" Millie asked, concern evident in her voice.

Eliza knew she had never allowed herself to look so weak before, but she was too weary to mind very much. "Yeah, I'm okay."

As they moved toward the door, Millie turned to her friend and lifted her eyebrow. "Would you really have stayed in there for another *whole* day?"

Eliza shrugged and grabbed her ratty, purple towel, letting it drag along the floor as she moved toward the door.

Millie rolled her eyes and let out an exasperated sigh. "You're such a liar, but I'm glad you're back. Are you coming to dinner after?"

Eliza shrugged. "Maybe. It depends on how tired I am."

"Okay, I'll try to smuggle something good out for you," Millie said, holding open the door and subtly offering her arm for assistance.

Waving goodbye to Millie, Sister Emily wheeled Eliza down another hallway while Millie headed to the cafeteria.

In the bathroom Sister Emily turned on the cold water for Eliza and hung up her towel on a nearby peg. She looked at Eliza as if wanting to offer more assistance, then nodded and exited the bathroom.

Eliza pulled the flimsy, yellowed-curtain along the rusty metal pole. Hidden from view, she began to peel off her urine and sweat-soaked clothing, dropping each piece to the damp floor. Her stomach growled so loudly she could hear it over the splash of water hitting the pink floor tiles. Stepping gingerly into the waterfall, Eliza savored the feel of clean water against her skin. She wanted to indulge herself for hours, but the water pressure often died quickly, and she wanted to get the urine off her legs.

Mechanically she lathered and washed her hair, then scrubbed her skin repeatedly with her thin bar of soap until her legs turned red and raw from her efforts. Feeling clean at last, Eliza raised her face to the cool stream and squeezed her eyes shut, ready to enjoy the last few minutes. Seconds later the water abruptly shut off.

Eliza sighed, wrapped her thin towel around her body and rung her hair out over the drain. Pulling the curtain back, she bent to gather her clothes and stopped short, realizing they were gone. The door opened and Sister Emily poked her head in.

"I hope you don't mind. I took care of your soiled clothing for you so that you could just return to your room," the nun said. Eliza nodded as she hugged the towel tighter against her body. She wanted to thank the kind nun, but she couldn't make her tongue form the correct syllables.

Sister Emily smiled. "Come on, let's get you into bed." She waited for Eliza to exit the bathroom and sit down in the cleaned wheelchair, then pushed her back to the girls' room. This time she opened the door for Eliza.

"Thank you," Eliza managed to choke out, surprised again how much the simple assistance meant to her.

"You're welcome, Miss Eliza," Sister Emily said quietly. "Now, hop into bed and go to sleep. You'll need to rest after your stay in the box. I'll be back with something from the kitchen."

Eliza entered her room and stopped short at the sight of red and brown objects on her pillow. An apple and a giant chocolate chip cookie. Questioningly she looked back at Sister Emily's retreating figure. As if sensing her stare, the nun glanced back over her shoulder, winked, and rounded a corner in the hallway.

Smiling, Eliza let the door click shut, walked to her bed and picked up the large treat. She pressed it to her nose and inhaled the rich chocolate scent. It was selfish, but she hoped the sweet nun would always stay at St. Agatha's. Everyone knew Sister Emily had grown up at the orphanage. The nun was just as trapped as the rest of them, but having her there made it easier for Eliza.

For the next twenty-four hours Eliza slept, her sore body working hard to heal her stiff joints and ligaments. Every few hours, she would wake and find a new treat or food item on her bedside table, put there by either Millie or Sister Emily.

It was Sunday morning before Eliza woke feeling refreshed and energized enough to rejoin the rest of the girls.

Entering the cafeteria, she noticed with a grimace that Matron Criggs was still eating, her plate half-full of scrambled eggs. The black smile leapt to the forefront of her mind and Eliza wished she had another bottle of ink on her.

Matron Criggs put down her fork and eyed Eliza as she moved toward her seat. "Did you enjoy your little vacation?" the headmistress sneered.

Eliza exhaled slowly and smiled through her clenched teeth. "I did, Matron. Thank you for asking." No matter what Criggs said to her, she wasn't going to react.

"Well, that's wonderful to hear, dear," the Matron laughed. Turning to the other nuns sitting beside her, she lowered her voice and added, "Eliza is such a *delicate* child."

The urge to push the Matron's face straight down into her plate of eggs was strong. Eliza would love to see the Matron locked inside the box for two days. She wouldn't feel so tough when that door finally swung open.

Feeling a sharp retort dancing on the tip of her tongue, Eliza looked up and locked gazes with Sister Emily. The nun wore a sad smile, as if to relay how sorry she was for the Matron's behavior. Eliza felt her anger deflate. If she angered the Matron again and was punished to more hours in the box, then all of Sister Emily's help over the past two days would have been for nothing.

Swallowing her pride, Eliza smoothed her plaid skirt. "Yes, and that is why I cannot thank you enough for the tender care that I receive from you. Enjoy the rest of your meal, Matron."

She may have the power to lock me away, but she'll never break me, Eliza thought as she maneuvered to the breakfast line with a genuine smile on her lips.

THE NEXT MORNING, Eliza and Millie sat in the dry field behind St. Agatha's in what was referred to as "the yard." It was a rare occurrence that they were allowed outside, but Adoption Day was tomorrow and Matron Criggs wanted the girls to look healthy. Usually

Adoption Day occurred once a month, but lately the Matron had struggled with finding interested couples. This would be Eliza's first since she had arrived at the orphanage.

At quarter to nine, the Matron had kicked the girls outside, announcing she was locking the door until dinner time while they put some color in their cheeks. Normally Eliza didn't mind escaping the confines of the orphanage, but today the clouds threatened a heavy rain and the wind was fierce. They all knew better than to ask to come in. Matron Criggs had left them out in a hurricane before, so a little rain certainly wasn't going to change her mind.

Eliza glanced at the towering shrubbery encircling the yard and wished that she was tall enough to jump over it. There were no toys, no swing sets, and no jungle gyms; nothing to help pass the hours away. Some girls played tag, others clustered together to avoid the wind chill. Millie and Eliza sat off by themselves near the edge of the yard. Millie didn't like all the yelling and shouting that came with yard games and Eliza had been banned from playing them after breaking another girl's nose during freeze tag.

For several days now, Eliza had been contemplating telling Millie about her plan to escape. She didn't want to go alone, but she knew Millie was delicate and feared she would say no. But Eliza had weighed the consequences. The worst thing that could happen would be to get caught, in which case Millie would be brought back to the orphanage and Eliza would go to juvenile hall. Eliza wondered if it could get worse than Matron Criggs.

Millie was humming her favorite tune, an old lullaby she had once told Eliza her mother used to sing to help her sleep. Eliza didn't know why the sound irritated her so much.

"Will you stop singing that stupid song?" she demanded, tossing a handful of dead grass at her friend.

Millie looked hurt as she presented Eliza with her carefully picked grass arrangement. "Sorry, Eliza," she whispered. "I won't sing it anymore."

Eliza instantly felt guilty. Millie was her only friend. "No, its okay, I'm sorry. I'm just mad that we're here."

"What do you mean?" Millie asked, already picking more grass.

"Aren't you tired of living here?" Eliza asked carefully. "Don't you want to just run away and start living your own life, where you can play whenever you want and you don't have to hide in fear of old craggle face?"

Millie shrugged. "Of course, but that's why tomorrow is so special. It's Adoption Day and if we pray hard enough, maybe a family will take us away."

"But what if they don't, Millie?" Eliza said. A new thought struck her. "What happens if you get adopted and I don't? I'll be stuck here forever without you." The thought scared her more than any punishment Matron Criggs could cook up. It didn't matter how hard the rulers hit or how dark the box was. All of that was bearable because she had Millie.

Millie carefully set down her grass arrangement and scooted closer to Eliza, placing her hand over her friend's. "Don't worry, Eliza," she soothed. "We'll find a place where we both belong. Where we'll be treated like princesses and will get to eat all the sweets we want!"

A small smile pulled at Eliza's mouth. If only a place like that existed, she would go there in a heartbeat. Millie smiled back at her. "And I will be surrounded by kittens!" she giggled. "At least twenty-three at all times. Little orange ones with stripes, black ones with white spots, and brown ones with bushy tails."

"Oh yeah, well when I grow up I'll be a fashion model and fly all over the world in my private jet!" Eliza giggled and the two friends dissolved into a fit of laughter just as the dark clouds overhead opened up and unleashed a torrent of rain.

Girls around the yard screamed as a boom of thunder sounded and ran for cover underneath the narrow overhang of the roof. Millie looked toward the orphanage, but they were too far away to even attempt it. Eliza pulled her back and motioned toward the tall shrubs. The girls ran for them and crawled into the dry leaves.

"Whoa," Millie cried. "It's pouring! Like Heaven decided to open up."

"Yeah, it sure is," Eliza agreed, testing how much clearance they had underneath the bushes before she sat up. "I'm glad these shrubs are so big, otherwise we'd look like drowned rats right now."

Millie glanced down at her soaked blouse and plaid skirt and smiled. "I'm pretty sure we're already drowned rats." The girls giggled together as another clap of thunder and flash of lightning lit up the sky. "How long do you think she'll leave us out here?"

"Probably until the dinner bell," Eliza said glumly. They'd all be lucky if they caught pneumonia. At least they'd be able to escape to the hospital for a few days.

The rain continued to hammer down on the dry grass, steadily transforming the parched field into a massive mud puddle. Matron Criggs would punish them for soiling their clothes before Adoption Day.

"What was that?" Millie cried suddenly, spinning around to look at the mess of branches behind her. Eliza peered as well, seeing nothing. "There it is again," Millie whispered, crawling through the brush and closer to the woods.

"Millie, what are you talking about?" Eliza questioned, following her.

"Shh, Eliza, it'll hear you," Millie warned, crawling to the edge of the shrubs.

"What will hear me?" Eliza demanded, not bothering to lower her voice.

"Shh! *That*," Millie hissed, pointing.

Craning her neck to get a better look, Eliza crawled as close to Millie as she could, but only the rain greeted her searching gaze. She scoffed and sat back on her heels. "There's nothing there, Millie. You're lying."

Millie spun around and shot Eliza a dark look. "No, I'm not, Liza," she insisted.

"Whatever," Eliza said, bothered by the fact that she couldn't see what Millie found so interesting. She began to wiggle back into the shrubs, but Millie grabbed her arm.

"Wait Eliza, maybe we'll see it again," she said, her voice hopeful.

Eliza hesitated, both curious and annoyed. Was there something out there? She considered her options for a moment, then decided to give in to Millie's curiosity. She wanted Millie to accompany her when she ran away, after all. She nodded at her friend.

Although the downpour hadn't let up, the girls left the shelter of the bushes and set off into the surrounding woods. St. Agatha's was situated in southern Louisiana, surrounded by miles of swamps and wetlands. The location had been chosen specifically for the landscape and designed to keep the girls within the grounds. Since the day she had arrived Eliza had heard the stories about Celia, the runaway girl supposedly mauled by alligators. It was the perfect cautionary tale: you run away, you die.

Eliza and Millie navigated their way through the woods, weaving in and out of bald cypress trees and hanging vines. After several minutes, Millie pulled Eliza down into a crouch and pointed forward once more. "There, do you see it?"

Eliza narrowed her eyes and peered through the falling raindrops until, at last, she saw something. A flash of silver light appeared to be dancing around the rain; up, down, and sideways it flew, captivating the girls. Suddenly another flash of silver burned across their gaze, this one much closer.

Disappointment made her smile falter as she recognized a silver dragonfly. "Is that it? A dragonfly?" Eliza demanded, annoyed she had allowed herself to waltz through the rain to see a bug.

Millie withdrew her attention from the faraway silver spot and looked up at Eliza. "It's not a dragonfly. It's something else," she insisted, once again pulling her friend closer.

Fed up, Eliza threw off Millie's grasp and crossed her arms. "No, Millie, I'm done. I'm cold and wet and mad that you brought me all the way out here to look at a bug." She began stalking back toward the orphanage.

"Eliza, please, wait! Don't go!" Millie yelled, stumbling as she raced after her friend. Eliza stopped as Millie ran in front of her. "Just hang on a second. I *did* see something!"

"Yeah, a dragonfly. Sorry to burst your bubble, but I've seen those a hundred times," Eliza retorted.

"But, Liza, this wasn't a dragonfly, it was something else, I swear," Millie cried.

"I don't know, Millie," Eliza said with another sigh.

"Come on, Liza. Trust me," Millie smiled. "The one you saw was a dragonfly but the other one...I think...I think it might have been a fairy."

Eliza snorted, now thoroughly exasperated. "A fairy? Millie, fairies aren't real. Stop letting your imagination trick you."

Millie crossed her arms and knit her eyebrows together in a frown. "It was too," she pouted. "I saw one and you saw it too. Just believe me!"

Another roar of thunder echoed overhead, causing the two girls to shriek.

"Come on, Millie, forget it! Let's just go back!" Eliza yelled.

A flash of bright lightning sizzled above them and Millie took Eliza's offered hand. As fast as they dared in the once more blinding rain, they ran back through the swamp until they reached the dry covering of the shrubs again. Peering through the leaves as they caught their breath, Eliza saw the girls and a few nuns still pressed against the brick building.

Sitting close to Millie in their drenched clothes, Eliza found herself glad this was the way life was at St. Agatha's. There would be nothing to miss.

The heavy rain continued, and the metal doors to the orphanage remained shut. Eliza guessed the Matron was hoping the browsing couples tomorrow would take pity on the girls if they were all afflicted with runny noses and coughs.

A few stray raindrops spilled inside their shelter as the wind changed course. Eliza shivered. If this was what she was leaving behind, maybe she would run away tonight.

The boom of the towering clock above St. Agatha's walls chimed the hour and Eliza watched in surprise as the doors split open, revealing a black hole meant to be their sanctuary from the storm. The nuns ushered the girls inside, staying low to avoid the fierce wind. Eliza glanced at Millie, ready to run for it.

Millie was staring straight ahead, her blue eyes glassy and lost in thought. Maybe Eliza was strong enough to run away right now, but Millie was not. With a concerned frown, Eliza reached out her hand and shook Millie.

Millie started and looked at Eliza. "What? What happened?"

"Criggs is letting us in now," Eliza told her gently. "Come on." She helped her friend rise to her feet and together they made a run for it as the rain overhead continued to transform the yard underneath their mud-slicked shoes.

CHAPTER

3

A S THE SMALL hand on the clock inched closer to noon, the orphanage was deathly silent save for the voice of Matron Criggs. "And furthermore, if I see or hear any of you complaining or whispering to any adult, you will immediately be placed in the box," she warned. "Always remember that we provide food, a roof over your head, and the necessary amount of interaction for you to thrive."

"More like to die," Eliza mumbled under her breath.

A few of the girls around her chuckled without averting their attention from the Matron. If they were lucky enough, today might be their last day under the titan's reign. Eliza smiled. Today was definitely going to be her last day taking orders from old Criggs, one way or the other.

"Now," the Matron continued, "the parents will be arriving in a few minutes. Once I have taken them for a tour of our wonderful orphanage, you will have two hours to meet and interact with them. As the weather is sunny and warm today, you will be kept in the yard. If a parent would like to adopt you, they will speak with me and we shall see what arrangements can be made. Have fun and remember to *smile*," Matron Criggs finished, emphasizing the last word.

Eliza knew the headmistress hoped that if the couples saw what a warm and happy environment the children were being raised in, they might at least donate money.

The girls were herded out into the yard. In unison they gasped. The dry, scratchy patches had been transformed into beautiful, soft green grass from the rain the night before. Numerous toys such as jump ropes, skip-its, hula-hoops, and dolls were scattered around the front door. The girls went wild, grabbing toys and shrieking with delight. Eliza scrunched up her nose.

"Where did all of these toys come from?" Millie asked, picking up a pretty doll with brown hair like her own.

Eliza pulled Millie out of earshot of the supervising nuns and plucked the new doll out of her friend's hold. "Don't believe it for a second, Millie," she pleaded. "Matron Criggs gave us these new toys just to make *herself* look good. Just you wait, as soon as the adults are gone, she'll snatch them all away until the next Adoption Day."

Millie frowned. "I don't know, Eliza," she said, taking the doll back and cradling it to her chest. "Maybe things will be different. Maybe the Matron will be nicer now."

"She won't, Millie," Eliza stressed, preparing to relay her plan for escape. "Just follow me and we can—"

The door banged open, and all of the girls stopped their games and conversations as they regarded the arriving adults. At least ten couples were filing outside—not enough for every girl to be adopted. Eliza was going to make it easier for them by taking herself, and hopefully Millie, out of the running. She looked toward her friend, saw her wide-eyed excitement, and decided to act first and explain later. She grabbed Millie's hand and took off running across the yard.

Eliza felt a sharp tug and cool air grazed her palm where Millie's hand had been. She stopped and looked back, spotting Millie a few yards back, sprawled on the ground. A young woman, probably around Sister Emily's age, was walking toward Millie, her hand outstretched and a big smile on her lips.

No, we're supposed to be avoiding adults, Eliza mentally screamed. She raced back to her friend, tempted to push the pretty woman away.

"Oh, my dear, are you all right?" the lady asked, crouching down to Millie's height.

Millie appeared speechless as she stared at the woman.

"My name is Olivia," the woman said, helping Millie to her feet.

"I'm Millie. And this is Lily," she whispered, holding up the doll she held for Olivia to see.

"Well, it's nice to meet you both," Olivia said. "My husband and I are looking for a little girl."

"Do you have any kids?" Millie asked excitedly.

Olivia shook her head and frowned. "No, we don't. That's why we're here today."

"Oh," was all Millie said, then spotted Eliza. "Um, that's my friend, Eliza."

"It's nice to meet you," Olivia said warmly.

"Hi," was all Eliza said, not trusting the woman's blue eyes and too-happy smile. Her other "mothers" had been nice at first too, all smiles and laughs. It only lasted for so long before the snarls and shouts rang out. "I'm sorry to interrupt, but Millie and I have to go somewhere," she added, stepping in front of Millie.

"But Eliza," Millie whined as Eliza took her hand firmly.

Olivia's smile faltered. "Oh, okay. Are you girls off on an adventure?"

"Yes," Eliza replied curtly and started to pull Millie away.

"Well, it was nice to meet you both," Olivia called after them. Without stopping, Eliza threw up her hand in acknowledgement and offered a little wave. She knew the lady was lying; her smile was just an act, just like all the others.

Once they reached the shrubs, Millie let go of Eliza's hand and looked back. "Eliza, why did you do that?"

Eliza tossed her long hair over her shoulder and crouched down to enter the swamp through the bushes. "Oh, come on, Millie, she wasn't going to adopt you. They all start off so nice but once you misbehave once, they don't like you anymore and they send you away. Trust me, you don't need her."

Millie looked back and Eliza followed her gaze. As if to prove Eliza's point, Olivia was now speaking to another child. Millie sighed. "Okay, so what are we doing now?"

"Just follow me, Millie," Eliza began, "we're going to get out of here."

"Get out how?" Millie asked, bending down and following Eliza through to the other side of the shrubs.

"We'll go through the swamp," Eliza explained, getting to her feet. "We walked through it yesterday without a problem, right? We can do the same today and this time, we won't go back! If we walk far enough, eventually we'll come to a road or someone's house and we can live together without the box, without hard beds, and without Matron Criggs! We'll be free, Mills!"

Millie bit her lip. "But Liza, we can't just run away. What about the alligators and Celia?" she asked, looking down at the doll. "I don't want to be eaten."

Eliza waved her worries away, striding toward the path they had followed yesterday. "Oh, Millie, that was just a story. Besides, I bet those alligators are dead by now," she scoffed. She looked at Millie sternly, her mouth set in a firm line. "This may be our only chance to escape together. That's what you really want, isn't it? Otherwise who knows what will happen. We could be separated. You, adopted by a family, and me, stuck here."

With a nod, Millie dried her tears and clutched her doll tighter. "Okay," she answered and without another word, the girls started off into the swamps.

They walked in near silence for several minutes; the only sound was that of Millie humming the familiar lullaby. "So, where exactly are we going?" Millie asked eventually.

Eliza swatted at a large curtain of moss and stopped. Pointing toward a sea of bald cypress trees, she said with a smile, "In that direction is a little town. Just think, in a few hours we could be getting on a bus and go anywhere we want to! And the best part is we'll be away from this place."

"Liza," Millie questioned, "how do you know there's a town out here? What if we end up getting lost?"

"Oh come on Mills, where's your sense of adventure? Yesterday you were thrilled to be out here searching for fairies and now you're acting like a scared baby," Eliza teased, smiling over her shoulder at her friend. "Just trust me, anywhere is better than St. Agatha's."

At the mention of the fairies, Eliza saw Millie perk up. "Do you really think there are fairies out here?" Millie called after her, excitement evident in her voice.

"No Millie, I just said that because that's what you were doing yesterday. They were dragonflies, remember?" Eliza reminded her, holding more moss to the side so Millie could pass through.

The friends grew quiet again until Millie spun around to face Eliza. "But what if there were fairies out here? What if I was right yesterday?"

"You weren't and there is no such thing as fairies," Eliza insisted.

Millie threw up her hands and Eliza stopped walking. "But how do you know that for sure? Come on! Please, let's just look around for a little while. We're already out here." She waited, and when Eliza didn't interrupt, she added, "If you do this and we don't find anything then I won't bring it up again. Please?"

Eliza looked away from Millie's pleading eyes and considered her proposal. All she wanted to do was get away from the Matron and the cold orphanage.

"Come on, where's your sense of adventure?" Millie teased.

Eliza turned back to face Millie, unable to keep the smile off her face. "Fine!" she grumbled, throwing her hands in the air. "We'll take a break and you can look for your fairies. But ten minutes, that's it, and then we keep going until we reach the town, okay?"

Millie nodded energetically, her smile threatening to split the corners of her mouth. "You'll see, Eliza. They're out here."

"Whatever, Mills," Eliza grumbled, striding away and sitting down with her back against the rough bark of a bald cypress tree. "I'll wait here while you look."

Gleefully Millie skipped off and Eliza closed her eyes, trying to think through a plan. She didn't have a very solid one, but she didn't want Millie to know that. She considered their options. They couldn't go back; Millie would be adopted, and if she wasn't, the Matron wouldn't let the girls outside any time soon. They had to run now, and figure it out along the way. It was a lot of pressure.

Suddenly Millie was back and shaking Eliza. "I was right, I was right! I found them!" Her usually pale cheeks were bright with color.

"You what?" Eliza mumbled, clearing her throat. "What did you find?"

"Fairies, Liza, fairies! Come, I'll show you!" Millie gushed, pulling Eliza to her feet.

Still trying to regain her wits, Eliza allowed Millie to drag her in the direction of the orphanage. Her friend stopped and pointed at the surrounding trees.

"There, Liza. Look," Millie whispered.

A minute or so went by and nothing stirred but the green leaves and tall grass as the wind drifted lazily by. Just as Eliza was about to lose her patience, Millie whispered something, her blue eyes sparkling. Frowning, Eliza followed Millie's gaze and saw it.

About twenty feet away a dragonfly was flying from branch to branch, but the longer Eliza stared, the more she realized that something was wrong. Most dragonflies flew in a jerky, haphazard way, preferring zig zags to straight lines. This one's movements were fluid and graceful. Eliza took a step forward, propelled by curiosity. The flying dancer took no notice of her approach. She could tell that it was mainly silver, but the creature's features were obscured by flickering black shadows that seemed to follow it.

Eliza glanced over her shoulder. Millie looked quite content as she watched the silver creature. Could this thing really be a fairy? Eliza turned back to face the dancer, but it had disappeared. Before disappointment could sink in, the leaves on a low hanging branch parted and the tiny being walked out on two tiny, beautiful legs. It had a torso, complete with arms, a neck, and a head.

Eliza blinked. Surely her imagination and Millie's mutterings about fairies were causing her to hallucinate. This couldn't be real, couldn't exist. She bit down hard on the inside of her cheek and felt pain; she was awake. But if she wasn't dreaming, how could this be? Fairies didn't just appear in the middle of a swamp. Didn't they live in enchanted forests or English gardens? All the fairytales she had heard at her foster homes had said as much.

Studying the tiny fairy, Eliza noticed that her petite body was covered in a shimmering silver glow that sparkled even in the shade. The black shadows that had obscured her vision before still wrapped and billowed around the fairy, but Eliza now realized it was the fairy's dress, not shadows. Even as the fairy stood still, staring up at Eliza with her pale silver eyes and smiling mouth, the little tattered dress floated and clung to the fairy like a plume of smoke, moving even when the breeze stopped.

Apart from her glimmering silver skin, there was nothing remarkably beautiful about the fairy. It seemed a bit dangerous, and Eliza instinctively knew better than to get too close. The fairy's wings did not resemble the petals of a flower like the fairytales claimed; this fairy's wings looked like a thick, knotted cobweb dragging behind the fairy as she tiptoed to the edge of the branch. The wings looked sticky to Eliza.

Footsteps crunched through the grass behind her and Eliza jumped. Millie had come to stand beside her.

"Isn't she beautiful?" Millie asked, her voice admiring. "I told you they were out here."

The two friends were silent for a moment as they stared quietly at the small fairy, Millie entranced and Eliza confused. "So...what now?" Eliza asked at last.

Millie shrugged and continued to stare as the silver dancer twirled on the edge of the branch and then alighted into the air with ease.

"Should we get going?" Eliza volunteered half-heartedly. By Millie's lack of response Eliza knew her friend wasn't paying any attention to her. "Mills? Remember, we were going to the town?"

Again Millie didn't answer, too absorbed by the fairy and her graceful movements. The closer Eliza watched it seemed as if the fairy and Millie were having a conversation of their own. Pursing her lips, Eliza saw the fairy open her silver mouth and throw her head back as if laughing, and a small tinkling sound reached her ears, like a jingle of tiny bells. Eliza was about to try and engage her friend again when the fairy flew over and landed on Millie's palm.

Millie's eyes grew wide as the tiny fairy danced and sashayed across her palm and took hold of one of Millie's fingers. Tossing her long, flowing silver hair to the side, the fairy laughed again and Eliza pressed her hand to her ear to block the high-pitched sound. Millie didn't seem to mind, not reacting even as the fairy gently placed her lips on Millie's outstretched fingertip.

Hypnotized by the impossible creature, Millie missed the flash of teeth as the fairy cradled her large finger in her hands. Eliza gasped as the fairy bit her friend. Millie jerked back with a start, her doll slipping from her grasp as she clutched her injured finger. A drop of bright red blood swelled to the surface and rolled down her finger, landing silently on the doll below.

Anger swelled inside of Eliza as tears formed in Millie's eyes. She moved to comfort her friend, but the fairy flew directly in front of her, blocking her path.

"Get out of my way," Eliza growled, ready to swat the fairy away. Even higher-pitched notes filled her ears. It wasn't loud in a malicious way, but it was enough to distract her and make her mind go fuzzy. What had she been so concerned about a moment ago?

The beautiful silver combined with the billowing black shadows of the dancing fairy mesmerized Eliza. She felt her eyes grow heavy as they followed the lithe movements and a deep sense of calm came over her.

A drop of blood rolled down the fairy's chin. Eliza shook her head to try and clear her thoughts. Millie had walked a few yards away, her dark hair thrown back and her arms extended, as if she were running them through something Eliza couldn't see. She attempted to call out to her, her voice sounding foreign to her own ears, and then a brilliant flash erupted before her.

Blinking against the sudden brightness, Eliza realized with a gasp that there were dozens, hundreds of fairies now, all dancing and singing their bewitching notes. The one with the red chin remained in front of Eliza, so close now she could make out features.

She had a delicate but sharp nose with high cheekbones and thin lips. Apart from the thin rivulet of blood running down her chin, she was void of color. The only thing that helped to break up the planes of her face was the shadows cast by the towering trees above them. Her pale silver eyes were unblinking as she watched Eliza.

The beautiful fairy was so close that Eliza knew she could reach out and touch the spidery wings. What did they feel like? Would they stick to her skin? She raised her hand and extended her index finger, curious to discover the texture of the strange wings. The fairy smiled and flapped her wings once, floating just an inch higher so that she was level with Eliza's approaching finger.

Taking hold of Eliza's offered finger, the fairy whispered something Eliza couldn't understand and ran her slender fingers down the length of Eliza's finger. Something in the back of Eliza's mind told her to watch out, to pull away, but the thought grew foggy and she couldn't pinpoint where it came from.

The fairy smiled again and Eliza felt her own lips pull apart in a similar gesture. A faint tickle brushed across Eliza's fingertip and she realized with joy that the fairy had kissed her. Her smile widened involuntarily as the fairy pulled back her lips and tiny silver fangs smiled back at her. She watched in a giddy daze as delicate teeth sliced into her fingertip.

The pain was brief, and Eliza's dark crimson blood bubbled to the surface of her broken skin in seconds. Breathing in through clenched teeth, Eliza pressed her thumb to the space just below the wound, forcing the little blood bubble to grow and eventually pop as it slid down her skin. Her first reaction was hurt. Why would the fairy do that to her? Eliza brought her wounded finger to her mouth and sucked on the tip, tasting copper. She looked down, focusing on her mary-janes.

I will not cry, she told herself.

More high-pitched notes wove in and out of her ears and the desire to look up suddenly became too much. Eliza raised her eyes to the sea of silver dancers laughing and singing before her. She felt her jaw fall slack.

The whole world had changed.

CHAPTER

4

THE ONCE LUSH and green landscape now resembled a winter painting. Every surface was coated in a fine layer of silver dust that made everything seem magical, untouchable.

Eliza took a step forward, enthralled with the silver beauty before her. Her shoes scuffed the grass, stirring shimmering silver powder that swirled into the sky like a miniature winter storm. Hypnotized, Eliza raised her hand to try and catch some of the beautiful dust but her fingers slid through. She turned her palm to check and noticed that her own skin was shimmering. Eliza watched, transfixed as the powder glimmered for a moment and then faded, disappearing as it sank into her skin.

"Isn't it wonderful?" Millie breathed, appearing beside her.

"Yes," Eliza agreed, her eyes roaming over the transformed land. The heavy moss curtains of the trees now resembled fine diamond blankets. She moved closer, marveling again at the swirling powder her steps created. Millie pointed, and Eliza realized that beautiful, exotic flowers were blooming as they moved, their vibrant colors of orange, violet and royal blue adding pops of unexpected color in the silver landscape.

Eager to explore the unimaginable world, Eliza reached for Millie's hand and the two friends took off, leaping through the sparkling grass until they reached a babbling brook. Instead of the frightening dark depths of a swamp, this little stream was crystal clear and ankle deep.

The girls sat down on the edge of the bank and removed their shoes, to dip their toes into the cool water. Below the surface, tiny golden fish darted to and fro and the girls giggled, submerging their toes and splashing one another. Eliza aimed a handful of water at Millie's neck and laughed with delight when her friend retaliated. The fight ensued until, thoroughly drenched, the girls lay down on the bank of the stream to dry off.

Eliza smiled as Millie stretched her arms above her head and brought them down to her sides repeatedly, as if making a silver angel. Water still sparkled across her friend's face and Eliza watched as a droplet ran from Millie's damp hairline onto her cheek and then fell onto the silver grass. Once the water hit the soft powder, it swelled and filled with the enchanting color, never dissolving.

A chorus of high-pitched bells surrounded the girls, and they sat up curiously. From every direction, beautiful silver fairies dressed in black, shadowy shrouds of cloth appeared, all sporting a pair of spidery wings.

The fairies landed with soft pitter-patters, like rain hitting the earth. They began to sing and chatter in an unknown language, but the sweet melody made Eliza smile. Around the girls tiny yellow daisies began to bloom, giving off an intoxicating aroma.

The fairies wasted no time in plucking the delicate flowers and fluttering around the girls. Without ceasing their sweet songs, they set to work weaving and braiding the tiny petals into both Eliza and Millie's hair, their rhythmic movements calming and relaxing.

Eliza felt her eyes grow heavy as she swayed along to the fairies' voices. A tiny tug on the ends of her hair made her open her eyes and she gazed with wonder down at herself. All along her arms and legs where the fairies had walked and touched were glistening silver bursts. Curious, Eliza leaned forward to look at her reflection sparkling back at her in the stream.

Her once loose blonde hair had been braided to the side and hundreds of bright yellow flowers peeked out between the strands. Eliza turned to inspect Millie and felt a twinge of jealousy. Her friend's braid was more intricate, with even more flowers—and unlike her bursts of color, Millie's skin was a glistening pale silver. No matter which way her friend moved, the tiny silver faucets in her skin shone brightly. It was as if Millie had been painted with the silver powder and Eliza had merely gotten sprinkled.

The singing changed, and Eliza knew the fairies were instructing them to move. Millie followed them at once, and Eliza left her shoes behind to hurry after them. As they traveled through the realm to a new area not yet explored, Eliza was overcome with the sudden urge to dance. Laughing to herself, she began swinging her arms and leaping into the air, wishing that she too could fly into the sky and twirl.

Strange, Eliza thought. *I've never liked to dance before.*

Giddy and loving the way her muscles felt from the movement, Eliza smiled up at the fairies floating above her. Their song had quieted, and they watched her, unblinking. Up ahead, Eliza saw Millie slip underneath a tall weeping willow tree, its heavy branches covered in shimmering silver mist.

Eliza followed, ducking underneath the curtains to find herself enveloped in yet another part of the realm. None of the sunlight from outside could penetrate the thick branches, yet bright silver light glowed warm like a flickering candle as the girls and fairies gathered inside.

Eliza glanced over to where Millie stood a few feet away. Her friend was swaying to and fro to music Eliza couldn't hear, giggling. Eliza watched the fairies until from deep inside she felt the steady beat of drums and the piercing call of a violin as the fairies resumed their songs once again, this time with the tempo and rhythm rising and growing in strength.

No thoughts filtered through Eliza's mind; she only felt the rhythm of the music and let herself go, her body somehow knowing what to do. On and on they danced, lost in the pounding beats and eerie melodies. Vaguely Eliza realized that the fairies were offering her tiny sips of something sweet from shallow petals. She didn't question what it was, but drank, letting the cool, refreshing liquid slide down her throat.

It was like a rave, a party, an out of body experience, and Eliza loved every moment of it. She had never felt so alive and free; time didn't seem to exist inside the wondrous canopy. She lost all sense of time, captivated by the moment and movement.

Eventually both girls collapsed, weary. Millie was beaming, but Eliza felt disoriented as the music quieted. *What did we do wrong?* She licked her lips, tasting a slight remnant of the cool syrup the fairies had offered her. Her head felt heavy.

All Eliza wanted to do was sleep, but the fairies had other plans. A few descended from the towering branches carrying round emerald green objects, a stunning contrast to the silver world.

Millie opened up her palms and received the green fruit without protest, sinking her teeth into the soft flesh. Bright red juice bubbled up and dribbled down her chin, resembling blood.

Eliza's stomach twisted at the gruesome sight and for the first time she felt afraid. *What's happening?* She shook her head as the fairies offered her the fruit.

Millie stopped eating and looked over at Eliza, the fresh juice still trickling down her chin. "Liza?" she asked, her voice gravely from lack of use. "What's wrong? They just want to make you happy."

Eliza stared back at her friend. Millie's blue eyes were glassy, as if she was looking straight through Eliza rather than at her.

Tiny fingers suddenly pressed against Eliza's exposed skin and when she looked down, she saw dozens of fairies all staring up at her with blind eyes, whispering words she couldn't understand. As their delicate touches and soft voices floated around her, Eliza began to feel herself slip away once more, away from her thoughts and worries.

Again, they offered her the dark green fruit and this time, Eliza accepted it. Bringing the fruit to her mouth, Eliza glanced over at Millie once more. Millie was no longer looking at her, but tearing the fruit apart in her hands, the sticky red juice splashing down onto her legs.

For a moment, Eliza felt a twinge of disgust but couldn't understand why. More hands pressed the fruit firmly against Eliza's fingertips, encouraging her to take the first bite. Smiling uneasily, Eliza bent her neck and brought the foreign food to her lips, feeling the bumpy surface of the outer skin. She exposed her teeth and sank them into the thick outer layer until she reached the fleshy core.

Eliza could feel the juice erupt from behind her teeth and squirt out of her mouth. She was surprised to discover the green fruit had a foul, sour taste. From the way that Millie devoured the fruit, she had expected it to taste like candy. A horrible rotten stench radiated from the fruit, like rancid meat left out in the sun. She let the horrid fruit fall, and giant buzzing black flies swarmed as it left her fingertips.

This was wrong, terribly, terribly wrong. What were they doing in a place like this? Eliza propelled herself off the forest floor and grabbed Millie under her arms, wrenching her to her feet.

Millie looked bewildered as Eliza grasped her wrist firmly and ran. Throwing aside the willow branches, the girls sprinted, Eliza choosing a direction at random and blindly plunging ahead. If she ran hard and fast enough, maybe she could get them out of the fairy realm. But as she started to sprint she could hear the singing fairies follow, and began to forget why she was running.

"Eliza, stop! What are you doing?" Millie stammered, breathless from the sudden physical activity.

Eliza shook her head, desperate to clear her thoughts. "We have to get out of here, Mills. Something isn't right! Didn't you taste that fruit?" She had to focus on that frightening thought. Why wasn't Millie thanking her? Couldn't she see how strange that place was? Couldn't she feel that something wasn't right underneath all the sparkling silver?

"No, Liza! Wait, just wait, I want to go back!" Millie protested, trying unsuccessfully to break Eliza's firm hold.

Eliza ignored Millie and kept running. The silver landscape seemed endless, glittering and shining brightly no matter which way Eliza turned. Pausing for a minute, Eliza glanced around, trying to locate the towering shrubs that lined St. Agatha's property. They hadn't walked that far, had they? She spun around, looking for any sign of the exit to the realm. Nothing but thin, glistening trees greeted her search.

Suddenly a loud hissing sound echoed all around them, reverberating off the trees and the shallow stream. Eliza looked down at their bare feet, terrified that they had stepped into a snake's den. But instead of a sleek, coiling body, Eliza's frightened gaze was filled with hundreds of fairies. Some were on the ground, their tiny hands wrapped around Millie's ankles while others were airborne, clinging to any piece of clothing they could secure in their small fists. No fairies touched Eliza. She watched with a sinking heart as peace filled Millie's face and she turned to follow the call of the singing fairies.

Fighting the effect the heavy melodies cast over her, Eliza struggled to remain in control of her mind. With all the strength she could muster, she grabbed Millie by the shoulders, breaking the fairies' hold on her and slamming her friend to the ground.

Eliza closed her eyes from the force of the impact and a dull pain began to throb in her shoulder. It was a few seconds before she realized that the air around them was silent. Hesitantly, Eliza opened her eyes and gasped.

No longer were they lying amidst the soft silver powder. Somehow they had escaped the realm and were back in the swamps, their bodies lying underneath the tall bushes that Eliza had been searching for.

To her right, Millie groaned and tried to sit up, untangling her arms from beneath Eliza's body. "What happened? Did we fall?"

she asked, confusion written in every line on her face. She shook her head to clear it, unraveling her braided hair and depositing tiny yellow flowers onto the dirt.

Eliza began frantically combing out her own hair. "We're safe now, Mills," she said, breathing heavily. Part of her was afraid to look back. Would she see the enchanting fairies again, their silver mouths all hanging open as they tried to call them back? Mustering her courage, Eliza peeked behind her and saw nothing but brown branches and a dark shadow of a large bald cypress tree a few feet away. Breathing out a sigh of relief, she turned to Millie and smiled. "It's okay now. Let's get back."

As much as Eliza hated the idea of returning to the orphanage, she was too rattled to try and leave again. The fairies might still be out there. Sure they were beautiful and intoxicating, but underneath their beauty lay something dark, something dangerous.

Eliza gestured for Millie to crawl out from underneath the bushes and back into the yard. Only the Matron knew how much trouble they were going to be in for disappearing for all those hours. Maybe they would spend more time in the box. Maybe a week this time. An image of the cold, musty box filled Eliza's mind and she shook her head. She would have to deal with it. It might give her time to think about all that had occurred.

Eliza rolled out from the shrubs and quickly rose to her feet beside Millie. In the yard outside the orphanage was a large group of girls and smiling adults, and Eliza recognized Olivia speaking with the same girl she had been when they left. They were even in the same position. It was too much of a coincidence. Had time stopped in the fairy realm?

"Come on," Eliza said, waving Millie toward a group of girls playing jump rope. "Let's get back before they notice us."

Olivia intercepted their path. "Well, that was a fast adventure," she said, surprised. "You weren't gone five minutes."

Millie stopped, looked back at the shrubs, and then at Eliza questioningly.

"Um yes," Eliza laughed. "It was a much shorter trip than we thought," she added truthfully.

Olivia smiled. "Do you want to play dolls with me?" she asked.

Millie glanced down at her empty hands. "Ah, not right now," she answered. "Maybe we can play with something else."

Olivia smiled. "Sure, I did see some checkboards over there."

Millie nodded. "Great, I love checkers." Olivia smiled and took Millie by the hand to the picnic tables that held the board games. Eliza waved her hand to pass and sat down on the green grass, watching the two play. *What just happened? How is Millie acting so normal?*

She closed her eyes and tried to remember the details of the past few hours, but every time her mind closed in on something as simple as the vibrant flowers, the image melted away. *Was it a dream?* Eliza shook her head. She couldn't tell for sure.

THE TALL CLOCK tower struck three and Matron Criggs appeared in the doorway. "Well, I'm afraid our time has come to a close. I hope you all enjoyed yourselves and had fun with our charming girls. If anyone is interested in speaking further, please visit my office."

Eliza joined Millie and Olivia as the large crowd was herded in through the double doors. The nuns directed the girls back to their rooms while the adults gathered in the hallway or headed for the front door. Olivia was among the three or four couples that remained.

Eliza paused and watched Olivia hug a handsome man and point in her direction. Happiness followed by fear squeezed her gut. Although she hadn't paid much attention to Olivia and Millie, she could tell they had both enjoyed themselves. *After two hours of playing together, Olivia wants Millie? She can't take her away!*

Making a quick excuse to divert from the group, Eliza snaked her way through the halls and navigated her way to the Matron's office. She could hear voices already talking inside. Quietly she snuck up to the door and saw with relief it was open a sliver.

Situating her body as close as she dared, Eliza peeked through the crack in the door. Olivia and her husband were already inside. Heart pounding, she listened.

"So, one of our little angels has captured your hearts," Matron Criggs was saying too brightly.

"Yes indeed," Olivia agreed.

"My sisters tell me that you spent a good deal of the day with little Millie and Eliza. Is that correct?" the Matron posed.

"I did, more so with Millie, but Eliza seems like a wonderful child as well," Olivia said. Eliza could hear the smile in her voice and felt a flush of warmth toward the sweet lady. She hadn't anticipated being adopted. Images of her and Millie helping Olivia make cookies in the kitchen bloomed in her mind. Olivia certainly seemed nice. Maybe this family would be different; after all, Millie would be there.

"Yes, isn't that nice. Were you interested in adopting both of the children?" Matron Criggs pressed. "Ever since dear Eliza arrived, she and Millie have been like two peas in a pod."

Eliza rolled her eyes. Matron Criggs did not attention to the friendships of the girls in the orphanage unless it benefited her.

There was a small pause before Olivia spoke. "That's so nice to hear, but unfortunately, we are only interested in adopting one child at the moment. We would like to offer Millie a happy and safe home with us."

Fear, anger, and a touch of jealousy swelled inside of Eliza. They didn't want her. Instead, they were going to take Millie, her one friend, away from her. She launched herself off the wall and ran for the stairs. How stupid of her to get her hopes up. *We should have kept running when we had the chance!* Now Millie was going to be taken away and she would be left alone, to face horrible Criggs by herself.

At the bottom of the stairs she collapsed.

Sister Emily came around the corner and stilled at the sight of Eliza hunched over. "Eliza, dear, are you all right? Are you hurt?"

Eliza didn't look up at first, ashamed of the few tears that had escaped. Sister Emily took a seat beside her as Eliza wiped the snot from her nose and stared at her wet skin. Was it just the snot, or was her skin shining? She shook her head.

"I just heard Matron Criggs talking with some adults and—and they are going to adopt Millie," she sobbed.

Sister Emily bent her head to look Eliza in the face and smiled. "But that's wonderful news, Eliza," she said. "She's your best friend, don't you want her to go to a nice home? Away from here?"

Eliza nodded glumly and wiped her face again. "Yes, but then I'll be alone and...and they didn't want me too," she admitted. "I just want it to stop happening. Whenever I make a friend, they get taken away from me!" Repressed memories began floating to the surface of her mind, snippets of past friends in foster homes. The details were foggy to her now. They had all left her. And now, the same thing was going to happen to Millie.

Sister Emily rose to the next step and wrapped Eliza in a warm hug, apparently unconcerned with someone seeing the physical contact. Eliza wondered if she looked that miserable. "There, there, it's all right. Is that what all of these tears are about?"

Eliza nodded.

"Oh, my dear, do not fret. A wonderful family has come for Millie and one will come for you too. Do not sit around being sorry for yourself, but happy for your friend."

A few more sniffles escaped. Eliza knew Sister Emily was right. The orphanage was a very unpleasant place to be and a delicate soul like Millie needed to get away. Eliza was tougher than Millie; she could hold on, she could make it.

Hesitantly she hugged Sister Emily back, fearful that she would reject her. Instead, Sister Emily pulled her in close and rested her cheek on Eliza's hair. "Don't worry, Eliza. One day, we will all get out of here."

A few minutes later, Eliza entered her room, all of her tears and jealous feelings left behind on the staircase as she greeted her friend with a happy smile. "Congratulations, Millie. Olivia and her husband are going to adopt you," she said as cheerfully as she could.

Millie glanced up from braiding her hair and stared at Eliza with wide eyes. "What? Are you sure? Where did you hear that?" She abandoned her braid and rushed to her friend.

Eliza stepped back from Millie's sudden attack, watching her friend's thin hair swiftly unravel itself. "I heard Olivia tell Criggs she wanted to adopt you. I was listening from outside her office," she explained.

Instead of the joyful celebration that Eliza had expected, Millie grew pensive and sat down on her mattress, staring into space. Eliza frowned. She had expected Millie to be elated by the news. Making sure the door was closed, she crossed the small room and sat beside her friend. Millie remained silent

"Millie? What's wrong? I thought you would be happy. Don't you want to be adopted?" Eliza asked gently.

After a long moment of silence, Millie spoke. "Of course I do. Of course I want to get away from here. It's just...I don't know. For some reason I feel like I have to stay," she explained, focusing her gaze on Eliza.

"Stay?" Eliza chuckled. "Why? In here is awful. You have a chance to get out and be happy, to have a normal childhood again."

Millie dropped her head and stared at her lap. "I can't explain it, Liza. Just...after today...I don't know, but leaving just feels...forbidden," she admitted. She looked at her friend again, and Eliza was shocked to see fear written plain across her face. *She's afraid of something! The fairy realm? Did it actually happen after all?*

"Mills, what do you remember about today?" Eliza asked hesitantly, covering the back of Millie's hand with her own. "What do you remember about the swamps?"

Millie scrunched up her nose and wrinkled her forehead as if trying to concentrate. "I don't...I don't really remember, it's all really hazy. I remember walking and then you fell asleep and I..." she paused, her jaw locking tightly as she tried to think. "Maybe I fell asleep too and I dreamed...I dreamed of finding...silver grass and sweet music," she managed.

Eliza nodded. Her own memories of the realm were fuzzy, yet she distinctly remembered feeling fear.

"I think we found something, Mills," Eliza whispered, dropping her voice low in case any of the nuns were nearby on their rounds. "I think we found something that we shouldn't have."

"Like what?" Millie asked, her blue eyes wide.

Eliza shook her head and gave Millie's hand a firm squeeze. "I'm not sure, but I do know one thing. I hope we never find it again."

"What about your plan to run away and reach the town?" Millie asked.

"Well, I don't need to now," Eliza said with a smile. "You're going to be adopted and I'll figure something out. In five years I'll be eighteen. If I haven't been adopted I can just leave and start my life then."

The thought of spending five more years under Criggs' iron fist made Eliza growl in the back of her mind, but the thought of venturing back out into the swamp and possibly back into the silver realm terrified her. She could deal with Criggs, but she wasn't sure if she could outlast the blind silver eyes and chilling songs that had haunted her thoughts all afternoon. She shook her head to clear it.

"So come on, be happy!" Eliza teased, tickling her friend. "Olivia seems really nice and I bet by this time next week, you'll have your very own kitten!"

Millie looked somewhat encouraged.

Eliza hopped off the bed and landed with a thud on the thin carpet. "Great, now let's head down to the dining hall. Hopefully there's something good leftover from lunch in case some adults are still wandering the halls." As she moved toward the door, she realized she was barefoot and paused. Vaguely, a memory flickered in the back of her mind and the thought of cold water raised the hairs on the back of her neck. With the distraction of Olivia, she hadn't noticed her shoes were missing. It was a bad sign that their trip to the realm hadn't just been a bad nightmare. She glanced behind her. Millie's shoes were gone, too.

Afraid to bring it up again, Eliza reached under her bed and grabbed her only other pair of shoes, a pair of brown flip-flops that had once been white. They were supposed to be shower shoes, but Eliza would have to make an excuse until she was able to swipe a new pair of black mary-janes. Quickly she located Millie's pair and lined them up in a neat row.

"Are you coming, Mills?" Eliza wondered, realizing that her friend had resumed staring into space. Millie's fingers had taken up braiding her hair once more, weaving and tucking the strands into place carefully. Millie had never worn her hair in a braid before today.

"I think I'm going to stay here instead," Millie said distantly. "I'm not hungry."

Eliza opened her mouth to say something, but realized she didn't know how to respond. Clearly Millie wanted to be alone. With a curt nod, Eliza opened the door and slid out into the hallway, leaving Millie alone. Her friend would be fine.

She has to be fine, Eliza told herself, but the uneasy feeling in her gut disagreed.

CHAPTER

5

A COLD WIND PULLED Eliza out of her dream and her skin prickled with the distinct sensation of being watched. Carefully she opened one eye and saw the sky was still a dark navy.

Something is there, Eliza thought fearfully. Her gaze swept the room. Something wasn't right.

The window remained bolted and shut. The dresser she and Millie shared stood quietly beneath it, casting a deep shadow onto the floor. Eliza looked at Millie's bed. The pillow and sheets were mussed and crumpled, but the bed was empty.

Suddenly something moved in the corner of her vision and a pale white object sprang before her.

Eliza opened her mouth to scream but a bone white hand crushed against her lips, silencing her.

"It's me, it's me, I'm sorry," Millie whispered, her bright blue eyes inches from Eliza's.

Anger and embarrassment flared. "What the heck are you doing?" Eliza said, throwing off Millie's hand.

Millie took a step back. Eliza pushed herself up and leaned back against the headboard, waiting for an explanation.

Her friend's lip quivered and her hands began to braid the ends of her long hair. "I'm sorry, Liza, but I saw that you were up and I was waiting and I just—I just—" Millie said.

Eliza sighed and brushed her hair back. "Just spit it out, Mills."

"I can't be adopted, Liza, please! You have to help me! You have to do something," Millie cried, taking a step closer to Eliza's bed. "I've just been thinking and thinking about it and I couldn't sleep and I just...I can't go!"

Alarmed that someone would hear Millie's raised voice, Eliza threw back the blanket and jumped out of bed, wrapping her hands around Millie's upper arms.

"Shh, someone is going to hear you! Do you want the Matron to find out?" Eliza whispered under her breath. "Just calm down, okay?"

Millie nodded, her breathing short and shallow as her fingers continued to braid. Eliza turned her friend and helped her sit on the bed, giving her arms a reassuring squeeze.

"It's going to be all right," Eliza said quietly. "I'll figure something out." She wanted to ask why Millie was more upset now than she had been last night, but worried Millie would panic further. She rubbed her sleepy eyes and took a deep breath, then sat beside her friend.

"Thanks, Liza," Millie said, sniffling as she leaned her head on the older girl's shoulder.

Eliza didn't reply, studying her palms as she thought. The first few rays of the sun were brightening the sky to a pale blue, giving Eliza enough light to see. She held her hands in her lap and frowned. Her skin was covered in shining powder. Glancing at her arms and the back of her hands, Eliza tried to figure out where the silver dust came from, but the rest of her body was clean.

"Hey, Mills, do you know what this is?" Eliza whispered, nudging her friend. Millie didn't answer. She was sleeping soundly against Eliza's shoulder, her breathing quiet and even.

Gently, Eliza maneuvered Millie onto the mattress. Pulling the blanket over her friend, Eliza noticed several small sparkles winking back at her. Two dotted the corner of Millie's eye and the others were sprinkled on her neck.

Eliza's gaze wandered down to Millie's arms and she gasped. Millie's arms, from her hands to her shoulders, were covered in the same silver powder that decorated Eliza's palms.

What is this? Eliza racked her brain, trying to remember.

The memory of swirling silver mist hovered before her as she pictured a bleached landscape, hidden within the swamp.

But that was a dream, we imagined it, Eliza told herself. But now she wasn't so sure. The silver powder, the missing shoes...and the strange way she couldn't remember any details.

They had been walking, they were running away and then... something had happened. Millie found something. Eliza pressed the heel of her palm into the center of her forehead. There were beautiful shadows and bright flowers. But there was something odd underneath it all, like a small scratch on an otherwise perfect mirror.

Frustrated, Eliza walked over to the window and stared out into the rising sun. The sky was streaked with colors, navy, rust, and fushia. It was going to be a warm day but Eliza shivered as she stared at the tall trees.

There was something out there, but the harder she tried to focus on it, the faster it slipped away. Exhaling, Eliza spun around and climbed back into bed, switching her thoughts to Millie. Her friend wanted her to stop the adoption and fast, but what could Eliza do?

Eliza groaned one more time and pulled the thin blanket over her head. It was going to be a long morning.

ON HER WAY to their first lesson, Eliza ducked out of line, pretending she had to tie the new mary-janes she had bribed Sister Emily for at breakfast

Millie glanced over her shoulder and gave her friend the thumbs up sign. It was time to get to work.

Once the group had passed, Eliza rose and quietly walked through the busy hallways in the other direction, dodging nuns and young girls, all who regarded her with raised eyebrows as if they knew something was coming.

Ready with several different excuses as to what she was doing, Eliza easily passed sister after sister by explaining that she was on her way to the bathroom, she forgot one of her books in her room, and she didn't feel well and was on her way to see the nurse. Each sister accepted the explanation given and told her not to dillydally as they moved on to their own destinations.

At last, Eliza reached the hallway where Matron Criggs' office was located and slipped inside an unused classroom across the hall, waiting for the signal to strike. Millie was going to create a distraction in one of the classrooms downstairs. While the Matron was called to the scene, Eliza would sneak into her office, find Millie's file, and hide it so that the adoption would be stalled, delayed, or perhaps even forgotten.

Not sure how long Millie's antics were going to take, Eliza situated herself on the floor to the right of the door where she would be able to spy on Criggs while avoiding detection.

To amuse herself while she waited, Eliza studied the small blonde hairs coating the back of her hand and arm. This morning they had sparkled like tiny diamonds, yet now there remained nothing to tie her to the frightening magical realm.

Eliza closed her eyes and the image of shimmering Millie greeted her. *Why is Millie still sparkling and I'm not? Was it just a trick of the morning sunlight?* Eliza let her head hit the wooden cupboard behind her as she tried to puzzle out the mystery. *It had to be my overactive imagination as a result of that dream.* There were no fairies hiding in the swamps.

Careful to remain low to the floor, Eliza crossed the small classroom and looked out the large window to the yard below. As she had predicated, there were no toys from yesterday, but at least the green grass remained.

Cautiously her eyes roamed to the tall shrubs. Eliza studied the bushes, wondering if she imagined a slight pull taking hold of her body the longer she stared.

In her dream, it had been fun dancing and singing with the beautiful creatures, but the unexpected glimpses of a darker world beneath all the glistening powder continued to plague her. Maybe she was imagining the scary parts, but the longer she stared, the bigger her doubt grew.

There was something there, something wrong about the fairies that was unsettlingly familiar. She closed her eyes and tried to pinpoint it, but the thought slipped away, evading her.

Abruptly her musings were cut short as a loud scream echoed down the hallway, followed by an abrupt shout of "*Matron Criggs!*"

The hairs on the back of Eliza's neck stood up and she quickly crawled back over to her hiding place. Pushing the door open a little wider, she made sure her body was still concealed from view before looking out. Sister Megan was rushing past, her heels clomping loudly in the empty hallway. She taught English. Eliza's heart beat faster. That's where Millie had been headed.

The nun skidded to a stop outside Matron Criggs' office and burst through the door.

"Sister Megan, what are you doing?" Criggs yelled. "I don't know what that other orphanage you came from was like, but here, we pride ourselves on manners and—"

"Please, Matron, you must come right now! The girls, one of the girls has hurt another one. I think—I think she might be unconscious!" Sister Megan cried.

Eliza heard the rough grinding sound as Criggs pushed back her leather chair and rose to her feet. "Is it Eliza Q? What has she done now?"

"No, Matron Criggs, it's not her. Please, please, it's Millie!"

"Millie? What happened? Who hurt her?!" Criggs demanded. The sound of scuffling feet echoed across the hall and the Matron shouted, "Sister, tell me!"

Eliza knew if Millie had been injured then the adoption would have to be postponed, along with the wonderful check.

Sister Megan choked on her sobs. "I should have been watching. I didn't see her grab them. I was writing on the board and then I heard a scream. I turned around and just saw blood and there was Millie standing behind her holding the scissors and.... and *smiling*!" she wailed. "It's my fault, if only I had seen her take them from my desk."

"Pull yourself together, Megan," the Matron barked. "You stay here and call an ambulance. I'll go see what's happened. Go, dial!"

Eliza heard the violent *slap slap* of Criggs' heels as she burst out of her office. For the first few seconds after the Matron left, Eliza sat in stunned silence. *Millie couldn't have hurt someone. She wouldn't stab someone, ever! It's not possible. My Millie isn't capable of something like that.*

Eliza flinched at the sound of Sister Megan grabbing the black phone on the desk and shouting into the receiver, relaying the accident and demanding an ambulance. She hung up, hurried out of the office and headed back toward her classroom. Eliza couldn't move. *This wasn't the plan. Millie couldn't have done this.*

Forgoing her mission, Eliza forced her frozen limbs to move and raced for Millie's classroom. There had to be a mistake. Millie was supposed to cause a diversion, but nothing like this. Reaching the hallway where the English classroom was located, she was greeted by chaos. Girls and nuns were crying and shouting, running and tripping as they attempted to maneuver around one another.

Eliza shoved through them and bumped into a girl in her class. She glanced down to where the girl had brushed her arm and was shocked to see a smear of red blood on her blue blouse. Goosebumps prickled Eliza's skin and a heavy dread curled in her gut. She bit her lip and leaned against a wall for a moment. What would happen to Millie if she had hurt someone?

Slowly Eliza pushed away from the cold wall and rejoined the hectic melee.

With steady, even steps, she moved toward the classroom, trying to slow the wild heartbeat pounding against her ribcage. At the threshold she paused and took a deep breath. Clenching her jaw, she was crossing into the room when a hand grabbed her by the ankle. Sister Megan was curled up in a ball on the floor.

The nun dug her fingernails into Eliza's skin, cutting off her question. "Don't go in there, Eliza," the nun pleaded, her face bloated and red from crying. "Please, don't go in there."

What could Millie possibly have done to get this kind of reaction? "I have to see if Millie is okay," Eliza said, her voice shaking as the nun refused to break eye contact. Gently she dislodged Sister Megan's grip and moved inside.

Numerous desks had been flipped and knocked onto their sides, and their contents poured onto the tile floor in scattered heaps. Posters that had once hung perfectly aligned on the walls had been ripped and shredded and the tidy organization of the English books had been destroyed.

Eliza's jaw dropped as she surveyed the damage. It took her a moment to realize a group huddled in the far corner. She stepped closer, crunching a pencil sharpener into plastic shards under her shoe.

Matron Criggs was kneeling above a girl Eliza recognized as Lacey, whose small body lie in a puddle of dark crimson blood. A large gash had ripped open her pale blue blouse and plaid skirt, snaking around her torso to her back. The Matron's face was as pale as the unmoving girl as she tried unsuccessfully to wake her.

A rustling sound, followed by a high-pitched cry, startled Eliza from her trance. She turned and saw Millie seated at the only upright desk in the room, two nuns standing guard beside her.

"Eliza!" Millie called out again, waving her friend forward with a bright smile.

Both nuns moved to restrain Millie and held her arms down with firm grips. "I was just waving to Eliza," Millie protested. "She finally came!"

Eliza furrowed her brow and remained planted where she was, shocked by Millie's casual behavior.

Millie cocked her head to the side and frowned. "Eliza? What's wrong?"

Eliza's words stuck in her throat as she stared at her friend. *Millie, what are you doing? Don't you realize what you've done?*

Someone bumped against Eliza and she fell to the floor as the school nurse scurried around her, toting every possible medical aid she could find. Without apology the nurse rushed to Lacey and began administering gauze to slow the bleeding.

Like that will help, Eliza thought darkly. She started to push herself back to her feet when her eyes alighted on an object several feet away. It was a pair of scissors, the blades separated and gleaming under the fluorescent lights.

Eliza felt her stomach turn at the sight of dark red blood dripping off the blades onto the floor. Was this the weapon Millie had used to stab Lacey?

"Liza? Liza, come here!" Millie said, her voice commanding like a bossy child. Eliza shook her head and looked away from the scissors, slipping on wrinkled paper and glossy folders as she tried to stand. She gripped a nearby desk for support, her body feeling like Jell-O. She looked again at her friend, not believing her eyes. Millie was surveying the commotion as though it were nothing more than a party. She smiled again at Eliza and waved, the motion restrained by the nuns gripping her arms.

The gruesome scene separating them was too much. The smell of rust and metal overwhelmed Eliza and she covered her mouth to keep from gagging. This had to be a dream, another terrible dream. Eliza closed her eyes and opened them again, but the same horrific dark red nightmare greeted her eyes. Millie called her name once more and Eliza could hear the hurt in it.

She raised her eyes back to Millie and swallowed. Millie's skin was still sparkling brightly like it had this morning, but there was no sun streaming in through the windows now.

Letting out a shaky breath, Eliza took a step toward her friend. Maybe it was all a misunderstanding. Maybe it was an accident. Passing Lacey's limp body she knew that her hope was the real dream. This terror was all too real to imagine.

The closer Eliza walked, the larger Millie's smile grew until, all Eliza could see were Millie's teeth as her lips threatened to split apart. Millie reached out a bloodstained palm. Eliza didn't want to take it and before she could refuse, the nuns restrained Millie again and shook their heads.

"Please, Eliza," one of them said. "Stay away."

Eliza nodded and remained a safe distance from the front of Millie's desk, her hands pressed tightly to her sides.

The restraint didn't seem to upset Millie now that Eliza had come over. "Thanks for coming, Eliza. We were waiting for you," Millie whispered, gesturing to her other hand.

Eliza followed Millie's gesture and frowned. At first, all she saw was Millie's other palm, a matching dark red. But then, the scene before her flickered and Eliza stifled a scream.

There, floating delicately next to Millie's hand was a silver fairy, no longer dancing and laughing. The creature was licking the blood off Millie's skin with her long silver tongue, the tips of her webby wings grazing Millie's exposed thigh.

Revulsion overwhelmed her as memories of the rotten fruit stench in the fairy realm wrapped around her, cocooning her senses like a toxic blanket. Retreating, Eliza's legs became tangled in an overturned desk and she fell with a hard smack onto the floor once again.

"Eliza, are you okay?" Millie asked, leaning over the lip of the desk.

Eliza shook her head violently, trying to shake the images out. "Millie—Millie what did you—how—what happened—why?"

Millie looked toward Lacey's slightly stirring body and frowned, as if coming out of a dream. "I had too, Eliza. You told me to," she replied calmly, and giggled as the fairy's eager tongue tickled her skin.

"No! No, no! Millie, why this? What did you do?" Eliza whimpered, her hands clumsily fanning out around her to try and put as much distance between her and her friend as possible. She had to get out, she had to get away from this version of Millie and the terrible creature with bloodstained toes. She needed to figure this out. She could no longer deny the trip to the fairy realm had been real, and somehow they had done this to Millie. The fairies were real and they were cruel and they would never leave them alone.

"Eliza wait! Eliza please, don't leave me!" Millie wailed, suddenly struggling against the nuns' hold as Eliza turned to go.

Eliza looked back and met her friend's terrified gaze. "Millie, please, look what you've done," she pleaded. In the distance came the wail of an ambulance siren, and she wondered if the police would come too.

In the flurry of flying arms and struggling bodies as the nuns fought to restrain Millie, Eliza watched the fairy, nothing more than a silver spark now, dart out from beneath the desk and vanish out the open window. Fear bubbled within Eliza's heart and she slammed her hands against her ears as the sound of the ambulance siren combined with Millie's wails to create a deafening scream.

She couldn't think, couldn't breathe. She turned again and raced across the threshold and down the hallway, not stopping until she reached the last place she ever thought she would go willingly.

She reached down for the small door handle, yanking and fighting against the lock until it finally gave way with a whoosh as the handle broke. Eliza leapt inside and pulled the door shut with a loud bang, cloaking herself in darkness as the emptiness of the box swallowed her.

A FEW HOURS later, Eliza sat in a gray room, the only furniture a metal table and two chairs. From above, a vent blew icy air down on her.

Eliza crossed her arms, trying to hold herself together as the pencil made sharp scratching sounds with every new letter Detective John wrote. She hadn't wanted to come. All she wanted was to hide away in the box for however long it would take to escape the frightening memories of that afternoon. But someone had told the Matron where she was hiding and without a word, Criggs had wrenched her from the dark box and pushed her into the back of a patrol car. The Matron had stared pointedly at her the entire ride, as if Eliza had been the one controlling the scissors.

Eliza bit her tongue, nervous under the detective's intense scrutiny. He had arrived in the room with a fat file that now sat on the table between them. "So Eliza. It looks as if you're familiar with the questioning process," the man said.

Eliza nodded. Every foster home experience had ended with an interrogation by the police. All of her past foster parents had accused her of terrible things, blaming her defiant attitude and unsavory personality for their personal tragedies. Eliza's case worker had assured her that they were just looking for someone to blame, but the damage had been done, and Eliza knew the fat file contained every complaint from her past.

She had no idea how long he'd been asking her questions about Millie for. *"Has your friend ever exhibited violent behavior before? Did she seem upset or agitated this morning? What was the relationship between Millie and Lacey?"*

Eliza shook her head in response to every question, wrapping her arms tighter around her torso. She didn't know how long they were going to keep her, or where they had taken Millie.

Millie had left with the police while Eliza was hiding in the box but she hadn't seen her since arriving. Eliza wasn't even sure they had brought her friend to the station. Detective John had changed the subject when she asked.

"Did Millie seem different at all the past few days?" the detective asked, setting down his pencil.

Yes, Eliza thought, but if she said it out loud, Millie would get in trouble. Eliza shrugged.

"I don't know. She started braiding her hair," she told him.

"Okay," John sighed, rolling his neck. "How about her attitude, her routine, her personality? Did she say anything about being angry?"

Eliza hesitated and looked away. *What can I tell him that he will believe? How do I explain what I don't understand?* "Millie would never hurt anyone, I promise," she whispered, chewing the inside of her bottom lip. "Something just...happened that was out of her control." She glanced at him, hoping it was enough.

John's eyes brightened. "Like what? What happened, Eliza?"

"I don't...ahh I can't explain it," Eliza said, regretting her choice of words.

"It's okay, just try."

She had to lie. "It was after the Adoption. I found out she was going to be adopted and I told her but she wasn't happy about it. She asked me to help her, to stop the adoption," Eliza explained.

"Okay, okay," John nodded, picking up his pencil. "So Millie didn't want to be adopted?"

Eliza tilted her head. "Well, not exactly. She was really excited about it but then...she told me she couldn't go, she couldn't leave the orphanage."

"Why? Did the Matron say something? Threaten her?" John asked, writing furiously.

"No, she'd love for the adoption to go through," Eliza scoffed.

"So why was Millie upset then?" John asked again.

Eliza shifted in her chair. It was so cold. How much longer was he going to keep her in here? "She didn't want to go. She said it felt forbidden to leave," she replied.

"Okay, keep going, Eliza. Why? Why did she say that? Did she feel bad about leaving you behind?" the detective continued.

Eliza pressed her hand into her eye, trying to rub the aching pain out of it. She had no idea what time it was. It felt as if she'd been in that room for hours. "Maybe, I'm not sure. She wouldn't talk to me about it. I think there was something else, something she didn't want to tell me. Maybe she was scared she wouldn't like the new family?"

John exhaled and put the pencil down, rubbing his eyebrows. Eliza could tell he was getting tired too. How much longer was he going to question her?

"So, you think she was upset about being adopted so she hurt Lacey to what? Maybe stop the adoption herself?"

Eliza nodded enthusiastically. The detective seemed to understand this explanation. "Yes! I think she might have just snapped. She's never done anything like that before. I know she didn't mean to hurt Lacey," she insisted. "Will she get in trouble?"

John pushed back in his chair and gathered his papers. "I'm not sure, kiddo. I have to get with my partner and go over the scene again. But you've been very helpful, thank you. I know this wasn't easy to do." He walked to the door and pulled it open. "You want to get out of this room?"

"Please!" Eliza said, jumping out of the chair.

It was another half hour until the ugly green station wagon that belonged to St. Agatha's drove up to the front entrance of the police station. Matron Criggs was driving, her face furious as Eliza opened the back door.

"Don't sit back there, it's full. You can sit in the trunk," the Matron said as she adjusted her habit.

Eliza rolled her eyes but didn't retort. She just wanted to get back and crawl into bed. Walking around to the back of the car, Eliza gripped the dirty handle and pushed up. A terrible screeching sound ripped through the peaceful parking lot. Several police officers walking by glanced in her direction, painful grimaces on their faces.

Cheeks reddening, Eliza ducked into the car and slammed the trunk shut. As she climbed into the trunk, she saw why she couldn't sit in the backseat. Crammed into every available space were the toys from Adoption Day, headed back to the store. Eliza glanced at the Matron, several angry comments ready, but instead took a seat and fumbled in the dusky light for the seatbelt. Finding it, Eliza clicked it in but the lock wouldn't latch.

Why did I even try? Eliza sighed, letting the loose belt slide away from her body.

The old engine chugged to life and they started the long ride back to the secluded orphanage. As the car rode along the dark streets, Eliza stared, dreaming about a normal life. The brightly lit restaurants, the happy families walking along the sidewalk—they didn't know how lucky they were.

Almost an hour later, the old wagon pulled off the smooth road onto the bumpy lane that led to St. Agatha's. Eliza shuffled along silently in front of Matron Criggs as the pair made their way to Eliza's room. Eliza didn't see or hear any of the other girls and knew it must be late.

At last they arrived and the Matron ushered Eliza inside, withdrawing her keys to lock her in for the night. Eliza took one step in, expecting to see Millie asleep. The room was empty.

"Where's Millie?" Eliza asked.

The Matron's lips pursed and her eyes narrowed. "That is none of your business. Now, go to sleep." Criggs pushed her further into the room and closed the door with a bang. The sound of the lock being turned echoed, followed by Criggs' retreating footsteps.

Eliza spun and slapped her palm against the wooden door. *Where did they take Millie? Are they keeping her? What if I never see her again?*

What if I don't want to?

Puddles of dark red blood loomed to the front of her mind and Eliza shivered. More images followed: Lacey's still body and Millie's bright smile, and the worst, the tiny silver creature pulling the strings.

THROUGHOUT THE NEXT few days, Detective John and his partner Amy questioned the nuns and as many of the girls as possible while they monitored the daily activities taking place in the orphanage.

One morning as Eliza was eating breakfast in the dining hall, she watched as the pair of detectives went from table to table asking everyone if they had ever talked to Millie. The girls all gave the same answers. Millie was quiet and shy. She was always very nice. No, they didn't know she was going to be adopted. No, she was never aggressive before.

Eliza frowned, getting angry as the detectives went around in circles, finding no new information. Looking down at her pale eggs, Eliza had scooped another forkful into her mouth when she felt a whoosh of air along her bare arm.

"Hey, do you remember me?" John asked, taking a seat opposite her.

Eliza's fork clattered to her plate. "Yeah," she answered. *Please tell me Millie is coming home.*

"So, I know you've probably seen us around the past few days but I was just wondering if you remembered anything new," John said, his voice hopeful.

Eliza shook her head, disappointed. "No. Where's Millie?"

John looked away. "Ah, I'm not sure, but I'm sure she's fine." He smiled but his expression betrayed his confident tone.

"When is she coming back?" Eliza asked, staring at him.

"I'm not sure," John said, glancing away toward his partner. He tapped his knuckles on the table and stood. "Well, like last time, if you think of anything else..."

"Yeah, sure," Eliza said, turning back to her cold eggs. If he wasn't going to tell her the truth about Millie, then neither was she.

He would never believe it anyway, Eliza told herself.

A WEEK WENT by and still no Millie. Every morning Eliza woke up alone and every night Criggs shut her away, glaring at her like the whole thing was her fault. Eliza wondered if it was.

At last, one day when Eliza was running late to Math, she caught a glimpse of dark hair and pale skin. Sister Amy was leading Millie into a small room, far away from the rest of the dorms. Eliza ducked out of the hallway into the English classroom, unused since the incident with Millie and Lacey, and listened.

"Your probation ends tomorrow, young miss," Sister Amy was saying with a clipped tone. "Until then, the only way you can go outside is if the Matron personally assists you. I'll be back later with your dinner."

The nun's heeled shoes slapped the tile as she exited the room, the door closing after her. Eliza waited for the nun to walk past her, then raced over to the room that held Millie and knocked lightly.

"Mills, it's me, open the door," Eliza said quietly.

"Liza? Liza, I'm in here!" Millie yelled.

Eliza tried the door and found it locked. "Mills, open up, hurry!"

"I can't, Sister Amy locked me in," Millie said.

Stepping back, Eliza looked up and down the hallway for any sign of the returning nun and a shining object caught her eye. Hanging on the wall beside the door was a small gold key. *Unbelievable.*

"Millie, hang on I've got the key!" Eliza said excitedly. Fitting the key into the tiny lock, Eliza pushed open the door. The first thing she saw was Millie's bright blue eyes.

"Liza!" Millie cried, drawing her friend into a hug.

Eliza hugged Millie back for a moment and then disentangled herself. Closing the door, she looked at her friend. She looked just like the old Millie, but her pale skin still glistened softly.

Eliza exhaled in relief, but goose bumps prickled along her skin persistently. The frightening images were suddenly filling her vision, and she felt a little afraid as Millie stared back at her.

"Where were you? What happened?" Eliza asked, taking a step back.

Millie shrugged, spinning around and running over to the window. She grabbed onto the edge and tried to hoist herself up, but the ledge was too narrow and she slipped back to the floor.

"What are you doing?" Eliza asked. Millie ignored her and tried climbing again. "Millie! What happened to you?"

Millie sighed and turned back around to face Eliza. "They kept me at the police station for a night and then they sent me to a hospital, something with a flower name," Millie said.

"And that's where you've been all this time, at the hospital? Were you hurt?" Eliza asked as her friend turned back to the window.

"No, I was fine. They just did some tests on me," Millie said.

"What kind of tests?" Eliza asked, staying close to the door.

Millie waved her hand flippantly. "I don't know. They scanned my head a lot and showed me weird pictures," she said over her shoulder, picking up her hair and braiding the ends.

Did the tests find anything? Maybe coming inside had been a bad idea.

"Do you think they miss us?" Millie suddenly asked.

"Who?" Eliza said confused.

"The fairies. I wonder if they miss me," Millie whispered, staring intently at the trees.

So she does remember. "Millie, what happened with Lacey?" Eliza asked, cautiously. She had to know what Millie was really thinking, if she remembered the fairies or not. "How did you get the scissors?" she asked for the first time.

Millie wrinkled her nose and narrowed her eyes. "I already told everyone. The scissors were on my desk and the rest just happened."

"You're lying Mills," Eliza said softly. "Someone told you to cut Lacey, told you to make her bleed."

"I'm not lying!" Millie said, suddenly furious. She let her dark hair fall away from her fingertips, the long strands instantly uncurling to hang loose and wavy. "Why are you being like this, Liza? I didn't do anything wrong."

Astonishment and shock raced through Eliza's mind. She took a deep breath and put up her hands, trying to keep her friend calm.

"Relax Mills, I'm trying to help you," she said softly. "When I went into that classroom I saw something, something floating beside you. You were laughing and showed her to me. Did she make you hurt Lacey?"

Millie stared at Eliza, bewildered, her mouth half-open as though prepared to shout. Eliza waited, watching her friend's brow crease as she shut her eyes, trying to picture the scene Eliza had described.

"I...I don't know," Millie whispered through gritted teeth. "It's like a dream that I can't reach. There was music and dancing and yellow flowers but I can't..." Millie pressed her palms to her temples. "It all just keeps disappearing into shadows. I remember sitting behind Lacey, listening to Sister Megan talk about synonyms and the next thing I knew, I was holding the scissors and...and..." she paused, reaching, searching for the next few memories.

"What then Millie, what happened then?" Eliza encouraged, take a step closer.

"I heard a voice, a whisper, a bell or something, and then it all flashed like a silver lightning bolt and there was blood and screaming and laughter." Millie opened her eyes and stared at Eliza, her pale blue eyes cold. "And then I saw you staring at me, with fear in your eyes, and you left me. You left me alone." Her voice had gone flat, void of all emotion as the shimmering faucets in her skin seemed to brighten even more. All of the progress Millie had made recovering the memories vanished. Millie slid off the ledge and started to dance about the room, picking up her hair and resuming her careful braiding.

"Millie, Mills? Wait, keep going—keep remembering. What voice did you hear? Whose voice were you listening to?"

Millie continued to braid her hair, deaf to Eliza's questions. She began to hum a familiar lullaby.

"Millie? Millie, please!" Eliza cried, ready to try and shake her friend from the stupor. "Millie!" But the other girl remained silent, humming and braiding, humming and braiding as if Eliza were no more than a piece of furniture.

Frustrated, Eliza spun away from Millie and stared out the locked window at the towering shrubs. She knew beyond a doubt that the fairies were out there and somehow blocking Millie's memories, keeping the truth at bay. There had to be a way to help Millie, to make her see what was happening, to make her remember. If she could remember, then together they could figure this out.

Eliza pressed her forehead to the glass and exhaled as Millie continued to hum softly behind her, filling the small room with the sad melody. Eliza left the window and opened the door, checking to see if Sister Amy was nearby. It was time to go.

"Bye, Mills. Don't worry, I'll try to figure this out," Eliza whispered, but Millie wasn't listening. Slipping out the door, Eliza closed it and locked her friend inside, replacing the key on the small hook beside it.

CHAPTER

6

THE NEXT NIGHT at dinner, Eliza sat toward the end of the long table, distancing herself from the others. She hadn't made many friends at the orphanage beyond Millie.

A sudden clatter startled Eliza from her thoughts and she glanced up to find Millie's bright face next to her.

"Hey," Eliza said warily.

"Hey, Liza," Millie said, her voice cheerful as she took a seat on the other side of the table.

"When did you get out?" Eliza asked, leaning forward. She could feel all of the other girls watching them.

"About half an hour ago," Millie said, taking a big bite of the stiff meatloaf. "Sister Amy waited while I showered and then I got to change and now I'm here."

Eliza nodded.

Maybe the tests came back and Millie is cleared. She wondered if they could go back to normal, to how it was before.

Millie spooned in another few bites and glanced around the dining hall, waving to a few of the other girls. A few empty chairs away sat the younger orphan girls, giggling softly, seemingly oblivious to Millie's presence and her crime. Their innocence seemed to gradually diffuse the tension in the room. Eliza exhaled. *Yes, life can return to normal.*

"Liza?" Millie asked, taking a small bite of her hard dinner roll. "Would you miss me if I went away?"

Eliza cocked her head to the side. "Like you mean if you went back to the hospital? Of course."

Millie shook her head and seemed to fight with her fingers as they hesitantly hovered in front of her loose hair. She hadn't tried to braid yet. The silver glow seemed duller now.

"No," Millie whispered and let her half-eaten roll drop from her fingertips. "No, I mean like if I went away and never came back."

Alarm shivered through Eliza. She straightened her spine and put down her fork. She didn't know why the simple question made her nervous, but she knew she wasn't going to like what Millie was going to say next.

"Like...if I died," Millie continued, glancing away from her plate.

"Why would you say that, Mills?" Eliza questioned, reaching out and putting her hand close to her friend's, not quite touching.

Millie shrugged and her hands fluttered to the ends of her hair. Eliza could sense the confusion and frustration building inside her friend.

"I don't know...just something I've been thinking about lately I guess," she admitted.

Eliza frowned and pushed her dinner tray to the side. "Mills, did someone say something to you?" Eliza knew from the night at the police station that Lacey was expected to make a full recovery. She was still in the hospital, and Eliza had heard a rumor she wouldn't be brought back to the orphanage. Everyone was still wary Millie might snap again.

Eliza lifted her eyes and looked over Millie's shoulder. Two women that Eliza had never seen before were leaning against the wall. They stood silently, their arms crossed over their wide chests and their eyes fixed on Millie.

Millie shook her head, her forehead scrunching with a frown as if she regretted bringing the subject up. "No, it's nothing, just some dreams I've been having," she whispered, her eyes downcast.

Eliza wasn't going to let Millie off the hook that easily. "What kind of dreams?" she demanded, her voice stern.

Millie's head snapped up, her face showing surprise at Eliza's tone. "I don't know, Liza. They're always really dark and hard to see. But in them I'm dancing and there are lots of voices whispering around me and then they get louder and louder and...I die," she explained, her bright blue eyes staring back at Eliza. There was fear in them, but also a chilling emptiness that had lingered since their cruel trip into the realm.

"Do you think someone wants to hurt you, Mills?" Eliza asked cautiously, afraid that her question would either shut Millie down or work her into a frenzy.

"No, that's not what this feels like," Millie groaned, her frustration apparent. It seemed as if she was trying to solve a puzzle, but had only blank pieces left to fill in the gaps. "It's more like...a preparation for something, something big but I don't know what it is. Every night I've had the same dream and it keeps getting longer and more involved each time. Then—last night, I saw myself die. I don't know Eliza. I don't know what it means."

A shiver ran up Eliza's spine. *She's scared. She hurt Lacey, but she didn't mean to. She's just scared.* "It's going to be okay, Mills. You'll see." A strange sensation passed over her, and her skin prickled with goose bumps. She felt as if she had had this conversation before. "Nothing is going to hurt you. You're safe in here."

It had to be true. Eliza suspected the dreams Millie was having were sent by the fairies, trying to reach her delicate friend and call her back to the swamps. It didn't matter, though. Despite how alluring and powerful the fairies seemed, there was no way silver dust could disintegrate the sealed windows and firm padlocks keeping the girls inside. As long as they remained inside the orphanage, Millie would be safe.

Pushing through her unease, Eliza reached her hand out and patted Millie's arm as she stood. "Come on, let's go back to the room."

Millie smiled at Eliza, but it didn't reach her eyes.

"Come on," Eliza said with a light tug on Millie's arm, trying to lighten the somber mood.

Millie remained sitting and suddenly the two women by the wall were directly behind her.

"Millie will no longer be sharing your room," one of the stern women said.

"Oh, where is she staying?" Eliza asked the one on the right.

"They're keeping me in the same room—" Millie began, but the other woman spoke over her.

"That does not concern you. If you are all set with dinner, please return to your room and go to bed," the woman said brusquely.

Eliza eyed Millie but realized there was nothing she could do. "Okay, well I'll see you later, Mills." She looked over her shoulder as she left, watching the two women follow Millie to dispose of her tray and back to the table. They were going to wait to escort Millie to her room until after everyone else left.

Too bad I already know where it is, Eliza thought.

A FEW HOURS later, Eliza awoke from dreams of silver lights to a flash of lightning and the deep rumble of thunder. She pulled the thin, ratty blanket tighter around her and squeezed her eyes shut, hoping she'd be able to fall back asleep. The room was lonely without Millie.

Come and play little one, a strange voice whispered.

Confused and bleary-eyed with sleep, Eliza sat up and strained her eyes, erasing the silver images as the dream voice melted away to reveal her small room. Outside the wind howled and the old wooden window bounced in the frame. She was alone; Millie was in her own room now.

Yes, you're almost there, the same soft voice said.

Eliza glanced around the empty room. "Mills? Is that you?" She pushed off the covers and stepped to the floor. A cold breeze wrapped around her ankles, making her breath catch. It was cold in the orphanage but this was something else. It felt almost eerie.

We've been waiting for you, dear, the voice continued. Eliza could hear the smile in it.

The overwhelming sense of déjà vu frightened her. Eliza threw open her door and raced for Millie's room.

Something is wrong, something bad is happening, Eliza told herself, picking up the pace as she rounded the corner down another hallway. Millie's room was all the way on the other side of the orphanage, well away from the other girls. She sprinted down the hallway that held the math classrooms, stopping at the last door on the right. Catching her breath, she was relieved to find the small golden key still hanging on the hook beside the door.

"Millie, it's me," she whispered and gently knocked on the door. With a gasp she drew back. The wood was freezing.

The same sense of dread that Eliza felt in her room washed over her once more and she no longer cared about discretion. Grabbing the key, Eliza slid it into the lock and burst into the room.

Everything seemed normal. The numbing cold disappeared. Eliza took a step further, careful to keep the door slightly open behind her. To the left was the bed, Millie's small figure huddled underneath the covers.

"Millie, are you all right?" Eliza whispered, gently shaking her friend. "Millie, wake up!" She pulled back the covers and gasped.

Millie was not in bed. In place of her body lay two pillows curled and propped up against one another. Suddenly, a chilling gust of wind wrapped around Eliza's body and she looked to the window for the first time since entering. Rather than standing solid and silent, the sealed window was thrown open, inviting the night in.

Cautiously she approached the window, her bare feet shuffling along the wooden floorboards. Her toes collided with something sharp that scuffed against the floor. Bending down, Eliza retrieved a large, jagged glass shard from the dozen or so that littered the floor around the dresser. Her brain numb, Eliza struggled to process this.

Leaning forward, she put the glass shard on top of the dresser out of harm's way, gripping the old wooden surface for support. It was unusually slippery. An alarm went off in Eliza's mind.

"What is this?" Eliza whispered, holding up her hand against the moonlight. Covering the dresser and now her fingertips were splotches and smears of dark red blood. Eliza jumped back in fright, wiping the blood off on the front of her white nightgown. *Where are you Millie?!*

Her gaze returned to the open window. She now saw that the window hadn't been opened, but broken, shattered to pieces to create the perfect opening. Someone, or something must have smashed it, fed up trying to get in.

Shivers and goose bumps bristled along Eliza's spine as she spun into motion. There was no denying it now. Eliza knew exactly where Millie had gone; she just hoped nothing terrible had happened to her yet.

Gripping her temples, feeling the fast pulse of her heartbeat race beneath her fingertips, Eliza scanned the room for something to help her. Anything she could take as she barreled back into the fairy realm. Other than the shard of splintered glass, there was nothing.

Eliza brushed the glass off the dresser, then boosted herself up and out the window. Rolling and falling to the ground, she jumped to her feet and sprinted toward the tall shrubs lining the edge of the yard.

After a few minutes of hard running, she reached the shrubs and dove underneath the long branches. Her ankle-length nightgown caught on the crisscrossing twigs and panic began to overwhelm her. Pulling and stretching and fighting in every direction, Eliza managed to break free and stumble out the other side.

In the dark, the trees loomed dangerously high, their long limbs swaying and reaching their wiggling twig-like fingers toward her.

Pushing her fear away, Eliza took her first few steps into the swamp, wondering how she was going to find the realm this time. Last time they had wandered inside, escorted by the fairies as they tasted their blood for payment. Was it going to be possible to find them if they didn't want to be found?

Eliza shivered and wrapped her arms around her small torso, fighting off the shivers that had nothing to do with the cold night. She could feel animal eyes watching her. She knew there were fairy eyes out there, too.

Choosing to proceed in a random direction, Eliza raised her foot to step over a large fallen log when an eerie melody wove through the trees, calling to her like a beacon. Eliza turned her head in the direction she thought the sound was coming from, and her gaze was greeted by the moss-covered bald cypress trees bending low and contorting under the bright moon.

Millie, where are you?

She spun in a slow circle, trying to pinpoint the intoxicating song. She scanned the obscure trees and their gently blowing vines for any sign of movement or flight that resembled a fairy. Her search came up empty. Taking a deep breath, Eliza headed toward the sound. The melody grew louder. She hiked up her long nightgown and picked up her pace, propelled by the gathering music and swell of voices. This was it. She had found Millie.

Ducking under another curtain of moss, Eliza charged through, anxious to find the fairies and her friend waiting for her on the other side. Her skin tingled with anticipation as the moss brushed past her with a gentle hush.

Instead of the large gathering Eliza had anticipated, the sight that awaited her on the other side of the curtain didn't differ from any other part of the swamp. A dark black pool of water leered at her from directly ahead, along with several bald cypress trees that stared at her in mocking silence.

But they were here! They were right here! Eliza screamed inside her mind, balling her fists into the wrinkled material at her sides. She spun back in the direction she had come, her heels sinking low into the damp earth. Her heart stuttered when she heard a definite splash echo behind her.

Casting a tentative glance over her shoulder, Eliza saw large ripples dancing across the surface of the black pool and stifled a choked scream. Something was in the water.

Instantly, images of alligators and impossible mutant creatures invaded her mind and she exploded back through the same mossy curtain, no doubt in her mind that a terrifying monster was hot on her trail.

In her hasty escape, her foot snagged on a raised root and her body went flying, sending Eliza stumbling and sprawling face first into a nearby tree trunk. She felt her skull hit the rough bark with a *crack* and slid to the swamp floor with a groan.

Almost afraid to feel for the damage, Eliza raised a shaking hand to her forehead and cringed. A thin rivulet of blood ran down her face from a small gash just above her left eyebrow. Flinching in pain, Eliza used both hands to ball up her nightgown and press it firmly against the cut in an attempt to stop the bleeding. The pain was blinding. She let one hand drop.

The blood continued to flow, the pain so intense it took Eliza a few minutes to notice another sensation running along the underside of her bloody hand. She glanced down to where her hand lay coated in blood and screamed. A fairy, identical to the one that day in the classroom, was licking the blood off her palm with hungry snarls. Eliza yanked her hand away and cradled it to her chest, horrified.

The fairy didn't seem to mind Eliza's frantic movements, using her long silver tongue to catch the last drops of blood dribbling down her chin before alighting into the air in front of Eliza, a curious smile on her blood-stained lips.

You've done well, a quiet voice whispered in Eliza's mind.

Eliza shook her head as a flood of choppy memories ignited at the sound of the fairy's words. Images of other children she had known from other foster homes blinked rapidly through her mind as dread overpowered her pain. That voice was familiar, almost comforting.

Come, it's almost time. You can even watch if you want to, the fairy's musical voice sang out shrilly.

The fairy darted away and the scenery before Eliza transformed, becoming once more the strange silver stage where only dark shadows and malicious beauty reigned. The loud singing, this time combined with pulsing drums, exploded in Eliza's ears and her confused gaze at last landed on the thing she had been searching for.

In the center of a large circle stood Millie, dancing and swaying and jumping to the hypnotic chants of the fairies. There were thousands of fairies, all dipping and hovering in the air above and around Millie as if they too were in a trance. Millie was bathed in the silver light of the moon and the fairies ethereal glow, shimmering like never before. The pure light caught the silver powder decorating her skin like a precious diamond.

Millie moved and danced with her eyes closed and a serene smile on her lips, her body flowing gracefully with the enchanting rhythm. Eliza gasped as Millie licked her exposed arms and silver fingertips sensually.

All around her, the fairies' chanting seemed to heighten in response to Millie's actions. Eliza sensed a dangerous hunger growing rapidly with the silver creatures. Something grand, and familiar was about to happen. The drums beat faster and the circle of fairies tightened around Millie. Eliza struggled to remember what happened next.

You can even watch if you want to, the fairy had told her, a large smile on her lips. Eliza wasn't sure what the fairy had meant but she knew now that it wasn't going to be pretty.

Without another thought, Eliza leapt into the tiny circle and wrapped her arms around Millie, trying to shield her on all sides from the silver mouths and glowing eyes.

Immediately, the songs cut off and hostile cries and whispers surrounded them as the fairies barred their pointed teeth.

Move away, angry voices screamed in her mind.

Eliza held on tighter.

This isn't how it's done. Move away or suffer the same fate, the numerous voices growled ferociously.

"Millie? Millie, please snap out of it! Snap out of it, we have to run!" Eliza cried, grabbing her friend by the shoulders and shaking her. "Millie!"

It took a moment for Millie to respond, but slowly her friend began to come to life under Eliza's hold and her eyelids flickered. At last she opened her eyes and stared back at Eliza.

Eliza screamed at the top of her lungs and fell away from Millie with a muted thud as the wet earth swallowed her. This couldn't be real.

Instead of her beautiful blue eyes, Millie stared back at Eliza with unseeing silver discs. The lovely color had been completely bleached out and she resembled one of the fairies, with no pupils, no sign of humanity within.

"Millie?" Eliza whispered, afraid to move or run. "Millie, what happened?"

Relying on her hearing now, Millie's head turned and angled downward to where Eliza sat on the damp grass. Millie titled her neck; her long brown hair was now streaked with silver and cascaded over her face.

"Millie, please, it's me. It's Liza. I'm here to take you back. You need help, Millie," Eliza cried.

Millie remained silent, but the angry fairies voiced their infuriated rants directly at Eliza.

What have you done? Get away, get out of the realm! The ritual must continue! You have done your part; let us finish what must be done!

The fairies snapped their teeth together, edging closer and closer to where the two girls waited. Eliza shook her head, desperate to stop the chilling words weaving through her mind. She rose and took a careful step toward Millie, reached out and took her friend's hand in hers.

"Millie, I need you to run. I need you to trust me," Eliza whispered, scanning the area around them for any sign of an escape back to the orphanage. The shrubs were nowhere in sight but that didn't matter. They would do what they did last time, run until they made it out.

Don't take her, Eliza. You know what will happen if you try. You do this every time. Just get away from her!

"Now! Run Mills!" Eliza screamed, shouting over the hundreds of voices pouring through her. She dashed through the thick screen of silver bodies blocking them in, keeping a firm grip on Millie.

Eliza propelled the two of them through the silver realm, joy filling her as she realized the fairies weren't swarming after them. The feeling was abruptly diminished by the sudden weight of dread dropping into her stomach.

Eliza looked back at her friend. A few fairies trailed behind her, suspended in the air like brilliant silver stars. Fear clutched Eliza's heart as the fairies whispered once more in her head.

We told you, Eliza. Say goodbye to your friend. The poison cannot be stopped; they said, their lips pulling back wickedly to reveal needle-like teeth.

Eliza looked around for any sign of an approaching attacker, her eyes settling at last on Millie. Her blind friend was staring at her with an odd expression, like an animal sniffing the air for prey.

Fear made Eliza drop Millie's hand and she took a step back, the hair on the back of her neck spiking. "Millie?"

Without pause, Millie snarled viciously and lunged at Eliza, her hands outstretched like claws.

Caught off-guard, Eliza stumbled back and Millie collided with her, sending them both sprawling to the ground. The sound of gnashing teeth and rabid breathing filled the night air and Eliza struggled to fight her friend off her.

"Millie, stop! Stop it!" Eliza screamed, but her pleas did nothing to stem the aggressive onslaught Millie unleashed.

All around her, Eliza felt her skin shred and break as Millie's sharp nails sliced through it and the terrifying sound of clicking teeth became the new soundtrack as Millie tried to latch onto any skin she could find.

There was no way to get Millie off without hurting her. Eliza whimpered as she pulled back her arm and let her fist fly, connecting solidly with Millie's nose. The unexpected hit sent Millie rolling backward, giving Eliza time to jump to her feet.

"Millie, please, calm down!" Eliza shrieked as her friend righted herself and snarled like a wild animal in her direction. "Millie, no!"

Eliza's cries did nothing and Millie sprinted toward her with a frightening burst of speed. Eliza turned and ran as fast as she could, her feet somehow acquiring an unnatural grace, maneuvering over the sinking ground and treacherous tree roots. The silver foliage began to disappear, turning a natural green. Eliza kept running, desperate to find the tall shrubs.

Finally, after a hard five minutes, Eliza caught a glimpse of the orphanage roof line and relief filled her.

Her lungs burned as she inhaled the cold night air and her legs felt like rubber bands. Just a little further and she would be safe. The towering shrubs loomed above her and Eliza gritted her teeth and dove through, closing her eyes against the cutting branches and sharp leaves. Her body hit the ground with a solid thud and all of the air exploded out of her lungs with a giant *whoosh*.

Her body screamed at her to stop, but the fear of what was chasing her was stronger. Desperate to reach the open yard, Eliza clawed at the dirt and dead pine needles, pulling her body out of the swamp. Her muscles protested with the effort, until at last Eliza wiggled her torso free.

Pulling her legs out from underneath the shrubs, she felt a sharp pain stab her calves. Glancing over her shoulder, Eliza screamed as Millie's solid silver eyes flashed before her, along with her gaping mouth.

"Millie, no! Please!" Eliza cried, tears pouring from her eyes. It was too much, too much. Eliza had no more energy left to keep running.

Behind her, Millie continued to snarl and growl maliciously, pulling her back inch by inch under the cover of the shrubs.

Eliza grabbed at the earth in front of her, but the yard was once again dry and brittle and the hay broke apart in her fingers, leaving her with nothing but dust to hold onto.

"Help! Please help me!" Eliza bellowed at the top of her lungs, but the sound that came out was barely above a whisper as her fear overtook her. Eliza could feel Millie's sharp, jagged nails cut and slice into her bare legs as she was pulled further and further back under the shrubs. She envisioned the horrible death that awaited her on the other side.

Hurried footsteps slammed against the hard, dry earth.

Eliza looked up from the dust and saw Sister Emily rushing toward her, the police right behind her.

"Eliza?" Sister Emily called out. "Eliza!"

"Help me! Sister Emily, please!" Eliza choked out, sobbing, trying one last time to grasp a dead root or something to keep her from disappearing to the other side.

"Hold on! Just hold on!" the nun cried. She waved one hand wildly toward Eliza, motioning the police force forward. "Get her out! There, she's right there!"

Two officers sprinted ahead and grabbed onto Eliza's forearms, yanking her back. The surprise counter-weight caught Millie off guard and Eliza felt her friend's grip fall away.

The cops pulled her again and this time, Eliza kicked her feet and dug her heels into the dry dirt and launched herself out of the bushes, falling into one of the cop's arms.

"Help me, please! She's trying to attack me," Eliza shouted, her words tumbling out of her shaking body like a waterfall.

"Oh my God!" Sister Emily screamed, clutching her throat with her hands. Eliza turned in time to see Millie barreling out of the shrubs, rabid snarls pouring from her mouth, headed right for Eliza.

"Robins, get her!" one of the officers yelled and Eliza watched as another cop grabbed Millie from behind and tackled her to the ground.

Millie growled viciously, snapping her teeth and clawing at the officer's back. Another officer rushed in to help and together they were able to wrestle Millie onto her stomach and secure handcuffs around her wrists.

Sister Emily rushed over to where Eliza still clung to one of the cops that had pulled her out. "It's all right dear, it's all right," the nun said, running her hand down Eliza's tousled hair.

Eliza wrapped trembling arms around Sister Emily. Together they watched the officers struggle to hold onto Millie as they led her across the yard toward the orphanage.

Eliza glanced away from her friend and a heavy sobbed raked through her chest. It was her fault. The fairies had said it was her fault! She had made Millie become this terrible monster. She let the tears run freely, too upset to worry about looking tough.

"What happened here?" she heard a deep voice ask from behind them.

Eliza looked away from Sister's Emily's sleeve and recognized John, the detective who had questioned her. He knelt in front of her. "Eliza? What happened?"

Eliza pointed to Millie's retreating figure with a shaking finger. "They broke the window and she ran out here. I tried to get her back but they wouldn't let her go so I tried to take her. But then she attacked me! I thought she was going to kill me. Please just help her. Her eyes, th-they took h-her eyes," Eliza stuttered, her lips quivering.

"Shh, shh, it's okay, we'll get everything figured out, okay?" John said reassuringly.

Eliza tried to nod but ended up crying. The fairies had said the poison couldn't be stopped now.

"ALL RIGHT, HONEY, this might hurt just a little bit," the nurse said as she slipped the end of a needle into Eliza's shoulder.

Eliza winced as she felt the sharp metal slide between her muscles.

A few seconds later, the nurse wiped a wad of gauze over the small wound, smearing the round bubble of blood with the movement. Eliza's shoulder ached as the medicine entered her bloodstream. Swallowing the growing lump in her throat, she asked timidly, "How's my friend doing?"

The nurse threw away the used syringe and twisted away from her, so that only her bright blue scrubs met her gaze. "Ah, you know what, honey," she began. "I'm not sure. I think the doctors are still checking her out. But I'm sure everything is going to be fine." The nurse looked up at Eliza and gave her a firm nod as she gathered up her needles and other instruments. "Now, you have to promise me to feel better, okay?"

Eliza nodded, dissatisfied with the nurse's answer. She knew it had been a long shot but she needed to know if Millie was okay. Helpless to do anything else at the moment, she sighed and pulled the covers over her small body and snuggled down into the mattress. Unlike the beds at the orphanage, this bed was very soft and she could even play with little buttons that moved it up and down.

After making a few notes and giving Eliza one last smile, the nurse pulled an ugly turquoise screen around her bed and left the room.

Alone at last, Eliza lay flat on her back and closed her eyes, but no comfort awaited her in the black depths. All she saw were Millie's bright, unseeing silver eyes. She could hear the snarls and gnashing of her teeth as she attacked. *What have the fairies done to her? How do I save her? Is it too late?*

The sound of the door being opened followed by a pair of footsteps, forced Eliza to open her eyes and sit up once again.

The bright screen rippled as a pair of hands pulled it back partway, revealing Detective John and his partner Amy. "Good evening, Eliza," Amy greeted warmly, but Eliza could hear the sadness in her voice.

"Hey, how are you doing, kiddo?" John said, taking a seat on the edge of her bed. "Did you get all of your shots?" Eliza nodded, rolling her battered shoulder. "Good girl."

It was silent for a moment until Eliza gathered her courage and let the blanket fall to her lap, revealing dark bruises along her arms where Millie had grabbed her. "How's Millie?" she asked, praying that the detectives would be more helpful than the nurse.

The detectives paused for a long minute and Eliza noted the way they looked at one another. Amy opened her mouth to speak but John cut her off. "She's going to be okay, but, she won't be able to return with you to St. Agatha's," he answered, gently.

Eliza nodded and bit her lower lip. "Can they fix her? Give her a few shots like I got?"

"It's not that simple, kiddo. Millie isn't sick like you. Shots won't make her better."

"What do you mean?" Surely there must be something the doctors could do to fix this, to fix her eyes. Someone must have power over the fairies.

"Sweetie, your friend has been diagnosed with Schizophrenia," Amy said, walking closer to the bed.

"What does that mean?" Eliza asked, clutching the edge of the mattress.

"It's a term used to describe someone who hears and sees things that aren't real," Amy explained slowly.

"What are you talking about?" Eliza demanded, getting angry. *Millie isn't hallucinating! The fairies are poisoning her mind!*

John cleared his throat and gestured to his partner to step away from the bed. "Ah well, once the doctors were able to get Millie to calm down, she kept muttering something about...fairies," he explained slowly, his eyes never leaving Eliza's. "The doctors weren't able to get very many words out of her but what they did manage to piece together was that Millie thinks fairies live in the swamps."

Eliza gasped. Millie was telling the truth at last! "And is she okay?"

John shifted to the edge of the bed. "It's okay, kiddo, you don't have to worry. Nothing is going to happen to her now. The doctors have her sedated and although she keeps rambling, she's safe."

"And the doctors think that's why she's sick?" Eliza said, reading both of the detectives' expressions and body language. "Sick because she saw fairies?"

"Yes, pretty much," John chuckled, looking back over his shoulder at Amy.

"They think she's crazy—you think she's crazy," Eliza whispered. "You don't believe her."

John cocked his head to the left and raised his eyebrows. "Eliza, what's wrong?"

Eliza bit her lower lip and tightened her jaw. She was glad that Millie was safe and secure in the hospital, finally away from the dangerous fairies and their hypnotic songs, but now, when her friend had told the truth, no one, not the doctors or the detectives, would listen to her.

"She's not crazy," Eliza whispered through gritted teeth.

"What? What did you say?" John said, leaning forward to hear Eliza better.

"I said she's not crazy! There really are fairies out there and they are dangerous, evil creatures! We found them when we tried to run away but they tricked us, tricked her! They did something—*are* doing something bad to my friend—and you just sit there laughing at her!" Eliza shouted.

"Wait, are you saying you saw fairies too?" Amy asked, dropping her crossed arms to her sides.

John hopped off the bed and whispered under his breath for his partner to fetch the doctor.

"That's exactly what I'm telling you!" Eliza yelled loudly, throwing one of the numerous pillows at the detective. "You asked for the truth yet you're not listening! Why aren't you helping Millie? Some-one has to!"

Eliza heard the soft click of the door close as Amy escaped the room and she was left alone with John. He studied her, seeming unsure what to do or say now that his partner had gone.

Eliza gripped her head in her hands and stifled a soft cry, suddenly overwhelmed by a fierce headache. She wasn't sure where her anger had come from but right now all she wanted to do was find Millie and get back to their room at St. Agatha's. At least everything made sense there.

The door opened again, admitting an older man in a long white coat. "Hello Detective," the doctor greeted.

The short man made his way out of the shadows and into the light. He had peppered gray hair, a thick mustache, and square black-rimmed glasses. His voice was kind and he smiled at Eliza. "Hello dear. Why don't we have a little talk," he whispered, coming to stand at the foot of the bed. "That'll be all for now," he added to John in a dismissive tone.

"I have to stay with her. She's part of an investigation," John retorted, hooking his thumbs through his belt loops.

"And she's also a child who has already been through quite enough tonight," the doctor replied with authority. He raised his bushy eyebrows and tilted his head toward the door. "I will speak with you afterward, Detective."

With a curt head nod, John gave Eliza one last look and left.

"There now, my dear. Can I bring you anything?" the doctor asked, arching his brow.

"No, thank you," Eliza replied. Her stomach was already in knots; food would only make it feel worse. "Who are you?"

"My name is Eugene Bodin," he said as he took a seat in the small armchair beside her. "I have been asked to speak to you about your friend."

"Are you a doctor?" Eliza asked.

Dr. Bodin jiggled his head. "Yes, but a different kind of doctor. Instead of making sure your body is healthy, I examine the mind. And I just came from giving your friend Millie's head a check-up."

"The detectives said she was sick, that she had schaphrona," Eliza said slowly, the syllables feeling odd on her tongue.

Dr. Bodin smiled. Eliza noted his teeth were very white. "The term is *Schizophrenia* and yes, your friend does indeed have it."

"But they're wrong," Eliza insisted. "I've seen the fairies too! She's not making it up."

The doctor removed his glasses. "The mind is an amazing thing, Eliza," he began. "The imagination is so powerful that it can create things that aren't actually there. Did you see the fairies first, or was it Millie?"

Eliza thought for a moment, remembering the first time they hid underneath the shrubs. All she had seen was a silver dragonfly. It had been Millie who insisted it was a fairy. *Is he suggesting that means Millie made the whole thing up?*

"Well, Millie saw them first but after I looked hard enough, I saw them too," she finally admitted.

"But did you really see them? Were there really fairies there? Think, Eliza, think. Do fairies exist?" the doctor asked, his questions coming in staccato. "Fairies are a wonderful construct of the imagination, dreamed up when we are sad or lonely or see a pretty flower blowing in the breeze."

"But these fairies weren't pretty, they were all silver and black," Eliza shot back. She had seen the fairies, had been haunted by them.

"Your eyes saw what your mind created and wanted to see, Eliza," Dr. Bodin went on. "There are no fairies, there never were. Millie crafted an excellent illusion out of her imagination and described it so well, that you too thought you were experiencing a piece of magic. But the truth is that fairies are not real."

"But they are!" Eliza yelled back, her anger sparking once more. "I saw them, twice!"

Dr. Bodin shook his head with annoying patience.

"What about the dust, the fairy dust that covered her when we were in the swamp?" Eliza continued, ready to defend the truth.

Dr. Bodin shook his head again and frowned. "That was pollen, my dear, nothing more than simple yellow dust that coats the leaves and ferns this time of year."

"No," Eliza replied strongly. "The powder is silver, not yellow, and it doesn't come off when she showers."

Dr. Bodin pursed his lips and lifted his clipboard. He held up a plastic baggie that shimmered and sparkled under the bright lights. Eliza's breath caught in her throat. That was the powder!

"This was found hidden underneath Millie's pillow back at St. Agatha's after she hurt Lacey," Dr. Bodin explained. "It is silver shimmer powder, taken from the art supply closet."

Eliza's breath caught in her throat. That couldn't be true, it couldn't. "That's ridiculous. Millie doesn't steal."

"Denial is a very strong emotion, Eliza," he continued. "The mind may be so convinced of a lie, that the truth seems utterly preposterous when we are first confronted with it."

Eliza shook her head back and forth, her fingers clenching and unclenching beneath the blanket. "Her eyes, Millie's silver eyes," she threw back at him. "She's blind now because of them. Are you going to tell me that silver glitter did that?"

Dr. Bodin once more consulted his clipboard and Eliza smiled. Hopefully he was at a loss, stumped by her question. He shuffled a few papers and raised a small photo, extending it to Eliza.

Depicted in the photo was Millie's wrist. Eliza recognized the purple braided friendship bracelet she had given her, surrounded by numerous tiny cuts and scars embedded into Millie's skin.

"The practice is called cutting," Dr. Bodin said sadly. "When depressed, young children and teens will find an object and often slit their wrists or thighs with a sharp blade. They don't cut themselves very deep, only far enough to let the blood flow. Millie's cuts were made by an old metal ruler, also found in her room, underneath her bed. The ruler, as it turns out, contains lead. That is the chemical that the doctors found in her bloodstream and that is what blinded her vision."

Eliza pressed her hands to her temples once more, trying to force the ugly image of her friend's cut skin out. Lies, it was all lies. *I would have noticed the cuts, and she would have told me if she was hiding objects in our room. I can't have missed all of this.* None of it made any sense.

Dr. Bodin was telling her that Millie had been severely depressed and created hallucinations. *Was I a bad friend? Was I too wrapped up in my own desire to escape that place that I didn't notice what was happening to Millie?*

Deep down, Eliza knew Millie wasn't mad, or whatever the doctor called it. She had been a sweet, caring, and gentle friend who changed when they met the fairies. They were real and nothing the doctor said was going to change her mind.

"Before you come up with another excuse for your friend," the doctor said, interrupting her thoughts, "understand that people with Schizophrenia are sometimes able to hide it, even from themselves. They can live somewhat normal lives until a severe episode alerts outsiders to the truth hidden underneath. I don't want to turn you against your friend, Eliza. I just want you to understand the facts so that you can go on to live a healthy life, away from all of this."

Eliza let her hands fall and bounce against the mattress. "You mean away from Millie."

The doctor nodded sadly. "Yes, away from her. The only way to help Millie is to help yourself," he stated.

Eliza snickered and sat back against the small mountain of pillows, her amber eyes roaming everywhere but the doctor's face. He would never believe her either. She had been so sure that once Millie exposed the truth, help would come. The opposite was happening. The adults didn't want to deal with it, they didn't like strange.

After several minutes of uncomfortable silence, Eliza broke the tension. "They're real and if you don't do something, they're going to kill her," she said with conviction.

Dr. Bodin exhaled and removed his glasses once more. "Ah, Eliza, I was really hoping to avoid this." He waved a hand in the air, and the door banged open, admitting several doctors.

Eliza's eyes widened in fear as she realized they were there for her.

Scrambling out from underneath the sheets, Eliza jumped off the bed and ducked around one of the doctor's outstretched hands. The others waiting behind the first doctor were too quick and they surrounded her, grabbing her limbs and securing her in place as she watched Dr. Bodin come toward her with a full syringe in his hands.

"Sweet dreams," the doctor said sadly, plunging the needle into her upper arm.

Eliza sucked in her breath at the sharp bite the needle made, but her fear didn't last long. The drugs took effect and the last thing she saw was the dotted ceiling as her eyes rolled into the back of her head.

CHAPTER

7

BRIGHT LIGHTS AND a sharp, clean, smell greeted Eliza as she awoke the next day.

Slowly she pushed herself up onto her forearms and propped her back against the headboard, the one lone pillow doing little to cushion the hard metal.

The white walls were blinding and she blinked several times before her eyes adjusted. Unlike yesterday, there was no ugly turquoise curtain splitting the room. The small TV in the corner was gone, and the only window was fitted with thick black bars. And she was alone. Instead of the constant flurry of police and nurses plaguing her bedside like sharks getting ready to feed, Eliza was alone, and that scared her more.

Throwing the thin blanket to the floor, Eliza leapt down onto the cold tile and quickly crossed the short distance to the barred window. Judging from her distance to the courtyard, she guessed she was probably on the third floor of a building. The four bars in the window were made of steel, almost like a prison window.

The distinct sound of a key being turned in a lock made Eliza jump and turn. Hushed voices could be heard from beyond the small door on the opposite wall. Eliza looked down, realizing for the first time she wore plain white linen pants and a white long-sleeved shirt. If it weren't for her blonde hair, she could almost stand against the white walls and disappear.

The door opened and Dr. Bodin, accompanied by a younger doctor with dark brown hair, sauntered in. As the door clicked shut behind them, Eliza heard the heavy sound of a lock being turned from the other side. Goose bumps prickled along her skin. Wherever she was, she didn't like it.

"Good morning, Eliza," Dr. Bodin greeted warmly. "How are you this morning?"

Eliza felt her heart rate quicken as they approached and glanced around the room, looking for an escape.

"Where am I?" she asked, cautiously moving so the bed was between her and the doctors.

"You're at the Belle Rose Psychiatric Hospital," the second doctor said, his voice deep and husky.

"Psychiatric?" Eliza repeated. She knew what that meant. Something else tickled at the back of her mind. Millie had said they took her to a place with a flowery name after she attacked Lacey. "But I'm not sick. I don't need to be here."

Dr. Bodin cleared his throat and put his hands in the wide pockets of his white lab coat. "We know that, Eliza. We brought you here so that we could keep you under observation. To make sure that you don't suffer from the same malady that Miss Millie does," he explained.

"Where is Millie?" Eliza demanded, distracted by her friend's name.

"Miss Millie is in another part of the hospital, undergoing treatment and evaluation," Dr. Bodin answered.

"Can I see her?"

The two doctors exchanged a look and the younger one stepped forward. "Not just yet, Eliza. First, we need to be sure that *your* mental health is stable," he said.

Eliza wrinkled her nose and glared at the young doctor. "I don't need to be here," she spat.

"All right then," the young doctor continued, crossing his arms in front of him. "What did you see last night when you chased after Millie?"

It wasn't going to do any good. They had already made up their minds about her. "I told him," she said angrily, pointing over the doctor's shoulder to Bodin, "last night. I ran after Millie and saw her in the middle of a dance with hundreds of fairies watching her. When I tried to take her back to St. Agatha's she attacked me."

Both doctors hung their heads and the younger man cleared his throat.

A minute went by and neither of the doctors said anything. At last the younger doctor nodded to Dr. Bodin and rapped on the small door. It swung open, revealing more white walls, and the doctor exited.

Once the door had closed tightly again, Dr. Bodin looked at Eliza over the top of his glasses and sighed. "Fairies are not real, Eliza. The faster you get that through your head, the faster you can go home."

Eliza considered this. "You mean you want me to lie?"

"It's not lying," he said, briskly. "Fairies do not exist and they certainly don't go around bewitching young children. Now, you and your friend are causing quite a lot of trouble for the Sisters at St. Agatha's as well as the other girls. No one wants to adopt from an orphanage whose charges are violent and claiming outlandish lies such as fairies in the swamps. What I suggest..." he paused, cleared his throat and continued, "is that you re-evaluate your story and then we can go from there. But, unfortunately, until then, I have no other alternative but to keep you at Belle Rose until your mental health can be proven stable." He rapped abruptly on the door and exited, the door banging shut behind him.

Eliza let out the deep breath she had been holding and slowly unclenched her tight fists. They wanted her to lie. To turn against her friend and say she had made the whole thing up.

She crossed the room and went back to the window, peering through the thick bars. If she lied, then she could return to St. Agatha's and be free to live her own life in just a few years. That would mean abandoning Millie, leaving her alone when she had finally admitted the truth. *But if I stick to my story, I may be locked away forever and never get a chance at a normal life.* The happy strangers she had watched on the sidewalk the other day flashed before her.

But then Millie would be alone forever

The bright Louisiana sun streamed in through the glass panes, warming the room. *How could I enjoy my freedom? Knowing Millie is trapped here?*

The light blue sky mocked her. Somewhere out there lurked the swamp and within its moss-soaked trees, the dangerous fairies that had transformed her sweet friend. She didn't know how, or where to even start, but somehow Eliza was going to protect Millie and only together would they escape.

THAT NIGHT AT dinner, a muscular guard escorted Eliza to the cafeteria and pointed to a small table where two other girls already sat.

They looked to be about her age, but their blank expressions and strange mumblings scared her. As Eliza sat in her plastic chair, she glanced to the girl on her left, taking in the buzz haircut. She wondered if the girl had cancer or if she had wanted it buzzed off.

As if in answer to her question, the girl reached up and let her fingers dance along the smooth, almost bald surface. She moved her hand about, becoming agitated as her fingers grasped for hair that was not there. With a shriek, the girl began to claw at her scalp, her short nails somehow managing to nick the skin above her eyebrow even as nurses flew to her side. Two grabbed her flailing arms and whispered soothingly while another prepared a large syringe with a gold liquid.

Eliza averted her gaze from the struggling girl and made eye contact with the other girl at the table, offering a weak smile before stealing another glance at the girl on her left. Whatever was in that syringe had worked and the girl was no longer breathing heavily or trying to touch her head, but staring into space, her mouth agape.

Wishing she had something to distract her, Eliza fiddled with her fingers and tried to act like she was not watching the nurses as they applied a Band-Aid to the bald girl and escorted her away.

Eliza focused on the blonde girl across from her, noting she had large mismatched eyes, one green and one blue. Eliza smiled at her again and the girl waved back, wiggling her fingers slowly.

"So how long have you been here for?" Eliza asked quietly, unsure whether or not they were allowed to speak. The blonde girl looked slightly older than Eliza.

"Just a few months," the girl replied, with a strong Southern accent. "My mama brought me here after I broke up with my boyfriend," she went on. "I didn't handle him cheating on me very well." She scrunched up her nose and tossed her long blonde hair over a shoulder.

Eliza nodded and pressed her lips together. She had never had a boyfriend before and was at a loss for what to say next. She had hardly even interacted with boys outside of her past foster home families.

"But its fine, I guess," the girl went on. "It's not like it is terrible here and at least I don't have to see *him*."

As Eliza scrambled for something comforting to say, the pretty blonde pushed up the sleeves of the same white shirt Eliza wore and put her chin in her hands, elbows propped on the table.

Eliza felt her eyes go wide as she looked at the girl's pale skin. Long, angry red cuts and fresh scars crisscrossed and zigzagged along her forearms, forming a scarlet spider web on the white flesh. Her skin looked like the picture Dr. Bodin had shown her the night before of Millie's cuts.

The sound of high heels interrupted her thoughts as a nurse set a tray of food before her. Eliza glanced around and was startled to see Millie at the table next to her, hunched over her tray, her silvery hair hanging like a curtain across her face. Slowly Eliza pushed back her chair and moved to sit beside her friend.

"Hey, Mills," Eliza said tentatively, sitting cautiously on the edge of her seat.

Millie glanced up from her tray and looked toward Eliza. Eliza's breath caught in her throat. The silver-streaked brown hair that had looked so magical last night now resembled the hair of an aging woman. Millie's skin was pale and sallow, her piercing silver eyes clouded.

"Millie, what happened to you?" Eliza breathed. "Are you okay?"

Millie stared at Eliza for a moment and then resumed eating her macaroni. Eliza frowned at the unnatural grace for her suddenly blind friend. "Millie, it's me. It's Liza, remember?"

"No touching! Turn around and eat your dinner, please," said a loud voice behind her.

Eliza returned to her own table and picked up her plastic spork. Cutting her chicken was going to be difficult.

As Eliza and the other patients in the cafeteria ate, nurses began approaching the tables, distributing colored pills to each patient. Eliza watched the blonde at her table take two yellow pills, then open her mouth and move her tongue to prove she had swallowed it. All the patients accepted the medicine as though they were after-dinner mints.

A nurse sat a large red pill in front of Eliza. She examined it, noticing a small row of numbers printed on the wax casing.

"Just swallow it, dear," the nurse told her gently, resting her hand on her hip in a gesture that suggested no funny business.

"But what is it?" Eliza asked warily.

"It's to help you sleep. To keep the bad dreams away," the nurse said.

For a moment, Eliza thought about hiding the pill or chucking it to the floor. Before she could do either of those, another nurse came around behind her and grabbed the pill out of her hand.

"Either you take it or I will help you," the large man said.

Eliza didn't want to ingest the vile red pill, but was well aware she didn't have a choice. Obediently she took the pill from the nurse, placed it on her tongue and swallowed it dry, grimacing as it slid roughly down her throat. The man smiled and walked away.

Making a face of disgust, Eliza glanced over at Millie. There were two white pills next to her left hand. She wondered what they would do to Millie, what the red pill would do to her.

Eliza watched the nurses begin escorting patients away and pondered it. There were so many colors and quantities. Her eyes grew heavy and her vision blurred. She needed rest before she could figure this out. It was all hitting her at once, the chaos of the last few days.

"Millie? Millie, something strange is happening," Eliza whispered, struggling to keep her eyelids open. "Millie?"

There was no response and Eliza wasn't sure if she had spoken out loud or inside her own head. She wanted to turn around and look for her friend, but her head felt so heavy. She wondered if she would get in trouble for sleeping at the table beside her cold macaroni.

SURPRISINGLY, ELIZA FOUND that she was able to slide easily into the monotonous routine at Belle Rose. It was like life at the orphanage except she no longer attended classes. There were still other girls she could talk to, though she rarely did.

Eliza wished that she could talk to Millie, but the only time Eliza saw her was at dinner and by that point in the day, Millie's medication did a good job of hiding her friend away. Eliza desperately wanted to reach out to Millie but the longer she was away from both the swamp and her friend, the less real the whole experience seemed. After several mundane weeks, Eliza began to doubt her own story.

Eliza met with Dr. Bodin every other day. During each meeting the doctor would show her the evidence over and over again, pleading his case that the power of the imagination was stronger than the actual physical world.

At first, Eliza remained steadfast and loyal, repeating over and over again that the fairies existed.

However, as time wore on and the fearful memories began to fade, Eliza started having trouble envisioning the dangerous creatures and had difficulty piecing together the scattered images she remembered.

"But they were there," Eliza insisted during one session. "They were singing and spoke to me...told me things." She groaned, pressing her palm to her head. It was so difficult to remember.

Dr. Bodin shook his head. "No one spoke to you my dear. You and Millie created these beings to possibly escape the confines of St. Agatha's. These—fairies were an escape and the only reason as to why they became violent was because you were projecting your own fear, possibly of the Matron, or of never being adopted, onto them. They only exist within your own mind."

Eliza had stared down at her hands, recalling a time long ago when her skin had glistened. None of it had been real. It was just the pollen.

Gradually Eliza began agreeing with Dr. Bodin during the sessions, convinced that the fairies had been nothing more than a trick of the mind. The first time she agreed with him, the doctor's face lit up and he smiled widely.

From then on, Eliza noticed subtle changes in her daily routine. With her obedient and cooperative behavior, the nurses and guards began to give her more freedom. Eliza wasn't sure if they were rewarding her, but with their trust Eliza found that she was able to explore the halls unattended, stay outside for longer periods of time, and was even given an extra dessert every now and then.

Things began to feel normal, comfortable. It was still hard to talk to Millie, but Eliza found that she wasn't miserable on her own. They had been divided up into different groups for sharing sessions and Eliza spent her days doing physical activities and supervised projects. She rarely saw Millie outside of the dining hall.

Four weeks after she had agreed with Dr. Bodin, the test came. Dr. Bodin leaned forward in his chair and rested his elbows on the shiny wooden desk separating him from Eliza. "So, my dear," he said quietly, "what really happened?"

Eliza didn't hesitate. She had been over and over the facts in her mind and the doctor's logic was hard and undeniable. "I followed Millie into the swamp and found her having a nervous breakdown. When I tried to get her to come back with me, she became angry and I ran," Eliza said with confidence, her eyes never leaving the doctor's. The words seemed so simple and easy to say now. *Why did I resist for so long?*

"And did you see any strange creatures while you were looking for your friend?" Dr. Bodin pressured.

"No."

Dr. Bodin leaned back in his chair and flicked his hand into the air next to his head. "So, there are no fairies lurking in the trees? No strange beings trying to corrupt your friend?"

Eliza smiled and shook her head. "Fairies aren't real, Dr. Bodin. They don't exist."

SHE HAD ADMITTED it, finally whispered the truth out loud. The fairies weren't real, they never were. She and Millie had made them up, caught up in a silly game.

Eliza sighed as the big hand of the clock struck nine and her bright white room was swallowed by darkness. Eliza wasn't afraid of the dark. She closed her eyes and snuggled deeper into the mattress, pulling the warm blanket up underneath her chin as she rolled onto her side to face the window.

There was a full moon. She smiled as the pale light enveloped her. With a large yawn, Eliza allowed her mind to go blank, welcoming the carefree dreams that the little red pill bestowed each night.

But as the moonlight burned stronger and the night deepened, Eliza's sweet dreams changed.

Rather than the warm ocean waves gathering around her ankles, the clear blue water turned dark and opaque. Tall reeds shot up around Eliza's calves and the smooth sand underneath her toes transformed into thick, slippery mud.

The beach she had been wandering began to disintegrate, disappearing behind dozens of trees and lopsided hills. Eliza pulled a bare foot from the muck and started to climb the shallow hillside in front of her on all fours, her fingers sinking into the moist grass and cold dirt. Something wasn't right. Mud and grass quickly filled the space underneath her fingernails and the smell of worms and rain filled her nose. After the sterile smell of the hospital for so many weeks, the strong aroma of nature made her head swim.

Why couldn't she smell the beach, the salty air?

Eliza's jaw dropped as she reached the top of the embankment to a familiar sight. Surrounding her on all sides was the swamp that encompassed St. Agatha's. Dozens of bald cypress trees with their gently swaying curtains of moss blocked her view of the orphanage roof, but Eliza didn't need to see it. She knew where she was and what came next.

"No," she whispered, pressing her thumbs to the soft spot of her temples, trying to wake herself up. This wasn't real. Fairies didn't exist.

The warm breeze billowed her nightgown around her, and a sharp bite from a mosquito on the back of her hand caught her off guard. Eliza squashed the blood-sucker with her other hand, smearing both her stolen blood and the little black body onto her skin in a dark smudge.

"Great," she whispered, staring at the broken body.

Above her, the leaves and vines whispered as another breeze drifted around her. This time, Eliza heard a new sound.

Like shards of glass clinking together to create a wind chime, the eerie melody wrapped around Eliza's mind, transporting her back in time to when she had stumbled around the swamp looking for Millie. High-pitched voices rose and fell in unison, blowing around her like the wind, carrying her feet forward.

Eliza tried to stall her momentum by grabbing onto a nearby branch or raised root, but the objects she grasped dematerialized and her fingers wrapped around nothing but warm air. At last her feet slowed, and she found herself staring at the same clearing where she had found Millie. But this time, the person dancing before her wasn't her friend. She narrowed her eyes, the sense of déjà vu growing stronger the longer she watched.

Long blonde hair bounced rhythmically, threatening to fall out of the hair tie holding it up. The dancer was a child, no more than four or five years old.

The child offered up her palms to the dozens of fairies watching her hungrily, her amber eyes wide and pleading as a smile touched her lips. Eliza sucked in her breath. The child was her.

You were lost when we found you
Lost and afraid and we took you in, watched out for you
In return, we asked you for a simple favor
That you agreed to honor in blood

Numerous voices all spoke in unison, making Eliza's heart beat even faster as the fairies' whispers caused her skin to prickle in fear. This wasn't a dream, but a buried memory.

Every two years we need a sacrifice
Someone young and innocent to fuel our magic
You agreed
Never forget that you agreed
We will never let you go

Eliza's eyes widened in alarm as the younger Eliza raised her tiny arms even higher above her head and welcomed the fairies. Each one swooped down, their spidery wings twinkling as they dipped in and out of the moonlight.

Then, without a sound, the fairies each laid a quick kiss on the child's exposed skin, their silver mouths drawing a tiny drop of blood with every touch. Eliza's stomach flipped as the red blood trickled down her young arms, landing silently in the grass below. Young Eliza only smiled, the pain lost to her as she was welcomed into the realm forever. Finally, she had a place to call home.

She would spend her life repaying a terrible debt.

As if rehearsed, the fairies alighted high into the air as one, flying in graceful swoops and chanting their terrible melody as little Eliza began to dance again. She closed her eyes and moved her tiny feet to the sound.

Eliza moved toward her younger self, desperate to stop this from happening. Her hand clasped the small wrist, still slippery with blood, and the vision changed.

No longer was Eliza staring at herself, but at a little boy with dark hair and gray eyes.

He pulled away from her with an angry scowl, resuming the trance-like dance Eliza had just witnessed herself doing. As he danced, his dark hair grew in long black waves, stopping below his shoulders. His skin darkened in the moonlight, until a small girl with skin the color of cocoa danced in his place.

This time, the name came to Eliza instantly. Harmony, the little girl she had befriended at her second foster home.

The little girl's lips parted in a happy smile and she reached out toward Eliza.

Harmony had disappeared. They had been out playing one afternoon and the next thing Eliza remembered was waking up in the middle of the night, alone in the woods. The police had searched for Harmony but never found her. What was she doing here, in the fairy realm?

Harmony's long black hair twirled in the wind and wasted no time transitioning to a pale blonde. The long curls expertly wound around themselves, forming two braids that framed the freckled face of the next child. *This girl was taller with bright green eyes that never blinked as she stared at Eliza.*

Michelle, another ghost from a previous foster home. Eliza felt sick and her head pounded steadily along with the drums.

Michelle's numerous freckles gave way to sparkling silver skin and creamy black shadows.

You've done well, Eliza, so well

But you're starting to slip

To abandon us

You know what we need

You know we won't stop until we get it

It's time again

Millie's sweet face now swam before Eliza. Her eyes were still bright blue and she smiled at Eliza.

We need her too

You can't keep her any longer

You can't save this one

Eliza watched in horror as Millie's innocent smile exploded into a fierce growl and the beautiful blue of her eyes drained away to be replaced by an empty silver sheen.

"No, no please. Millie, stop this," Eliza sobbed, stepping away from her friend. All the other kids, her friends from the other homes, had this happened to them too? Had the fairies done something to block her memories, only to unleash them all now? If the images she had seen were true, then she did this. All of their disappearances, their deaths had been because of her.

No matter where you go

Or what you say

We will never leave you

Their chilling voices whispered loudly, cocooning her dark thoughts. As they spoke the last word, Millie lunged. The last thing Eliza saw was the bright gleam of her friend's eyes.

Eliza's eyes opened and she shot out of bed, trembling as the terrifying images, dreams, memories vanished. White walls and the monotonous ticking of the wall clock greeted her.

Eliza looked down. Her bare feet were covered in dry mud, her sheets filthy and black. It looked as if she had been running through the woods all night.

"No, no this can't be real. I'm still dreaming. Yes, I haven't woken up yet," Eliza informed herself, her voice shaking. She ran to the door and pounded on it with both fists. "Hello! Hello, can anyone hear me! I need to wake up!" she screamed. "Please, someone come wake me up!"

She heard the lock flip on the other side and the heavy door swung open to reveal her favorite guard, Leroy. "Miss Eliza, are you okay?" he asked, his dark eyebrows arched.

"Yes, yes," Eliza said quickly. "I j-just need you to wake me up. I'm dreaming and can't stop!" She pointed to the empty bed she had just left.

Leroy peered around Eliza and looked back at her. "But you are awake, Miss Eliza."

"No, I can't be, my feet..." her voice trailed off as she looked down. There was no longer any mud or dried grass clinging to her skin. "Wait, wait look at this!" Eliza ran backward and pointed to the bed, throwing back the wrinkled sheets. "Look, I was covered in dirt!"

Leroy looked and Eliza followed his gaze. There was nothing but the imprint of where her body had lain.

"Miss Eliza..." Leroy began, his voice hesitant.

"Please, you have to believe me! I was covered in it! It was here!" Eliza shouted, her eyes tearing up. "Just please wake me up!"

Several more guards and nurses rushed inside the room and held Eliza in place as another nurse prepared a long syringe. "Just relax honey," the nurse said as she moved to position the needle in Eliza's shoulder.

"I don't want to go back to the dark, please! Just wake me up!" Eliza screamed, flailing hopelessly as they restrained her. A moment later she felt the sharp prick of the needle bite into her skin. The room around her sloshed from side to side and she collapsed.

CHAPTER

8

"ARE YOU SURE you want to talk now?" Dr. Bodin asked, rubbing the skin between his eyebrows. "You don't want to wait until you've had a chance to calm down?"

Eliza shook her head, gnawing on her thumb so hard she tasted blood in her mouth. Something was wrong, something was bad. That hadn't been a normal dream. She had known those kids, played with them. She had taken them away.

"No, I need to talk now, right now. I can't go back to sleep." She paused her pacing and gripped the back of the upholstered chair she was supposed to be sitting in.

Dr. Bodin glanced at the clock, clearly weary of any conversation happening at four in the morning. "All right then, why don't you start at the beginning? What's been troubling you? Did it just start tonight? After our session yesterday afternoon you seemed... happy, joyful almost."

"I was! That's just it, I was! I was finally free of them but somehow they knew, they knew I was getting better so they brought me back in, made me—remember the bad things," Eliza cried, her thoughts running faster than her tongue could form them. "It was as if they wanted me to try—wanted me to try and forget, just so they could pull me back!"

Dr. Bodin wrinkled his nose and stifled a yawn. "Who my dear? Who wants to bring you back?"

Eliza stopped, the side of her thumb still in her mouth. If she admitted that it was the fairies trying to send her a message, then all of her progress and special privileges would evaporate. Everything she had been working for the past few weeks would be gone.

Dr. Bodin cleared his throat and adjusted his glasses. Eliza could see how tired his eyes were as they watched her. "Eliza? Who is trying to bring you back?"

Shaking her head, Eliza lowered her thumb and came around from the backside of the chair and took a seat. She couldn't admit what she had seen in her dream. If she did, they would never trust her again. "I don't know," she whispered, refusing to meet the doctor's gaze. "Maybe it was just a really bad dream."

A few quiet minutes ticked by while Dr. Bodin studied Eliza, waiting for her next move. At last he sighed heavily. "You know, Eliza the mind, as we have discussed, is a marvelous thing. When we need a way out due to pressures or stresses in our lives, the brain creates safe outlets where all of that restless energy can escape to. Perhaps this bad dream was your mind's way of telling you that you're not ready to give up the fairies." The doctor let his words hang between them for several minutes, his expression giving nothing away.

Eliza wasn't sure what he was trying to say. "So, you still think I'm mad?" she asked, her voice shaky.

"No, Eliza. I don't think that. But I do think that it's a good idea if we continue our daily sessions. As much as you want to believe the facts, I think there's a part of you that still truly believes the fairies exist."

Eliza remained silent, worried anything she said would cement that belief.

"Now, let's get you back to bed until breakfast time, hmm?" Dr. Bodin smiled and waved forward Leroy, who was waiting in the corner. "I'll talk to you later today, at our usual time."

Eliza nodded and rose from the chair. Leroy placed a hand on her shoulder to steer her out the door. Glancing back, she observed Dr. Bodin hunched over the file, writing something on a blank piece of paper. She could only imagine what he thought.

THREE WEEKS PASSED without much incident and her sessions with Dr. Bodin all began to blur into one.

As he prattled on about the mind creating strange fantasies, Eliza found herself hoping he was right. If it hadn't been a dream and she somehow visited the swamp, then there was nothing she could do to keep Millie safe. If the fairies could reach her from miles and miles away inside a locked room, then they could find Millie too and make her disappear like everyone else.

Eliza was being escorted to the lounge when a nurse stopped them in the hall. "Well Miss Eliza, I do believe you have a visitor today!"

"A visitor?" Eliza repeated doubtfully. "Who?"

"I think she's from St. Agatha's," the nurse said before turning around and heading in the other direction. "She's waiting for you in the garden," she tossed over her shoulder.

"Well, it's up to you, Eliza. Do you want to go see who it is?" Leroy asked her.

Eliza hesitated. *Who besides the Matron would visit me all the way out here? And why would the Matron?* Whoever it was, it had to be more interesting than staring at a Chinese checkerboard for the next hour.

"Sure, let's go." She smiled weakly.

They turned down a different hallway that led to the small enclosed yard often referred to as the garden. Towering brick walls lined the property but the flowers and manicured grass offered a nice escape from the bleak white walls.

Leroy led Eliza out through the large door and then stepped aside to where several other guards stood watching the patients. Eliza sighed mentally. One dream and she was back to being watched like a hawk.

"Eliza?" a quiet voice called.

Eliza glanced over her left shoulder. Sitting on a small stone bench was Sister Emily, clad in the usual gray dress and habit that she wore at the orphanage. Eliza's smile widened.

"Sister Emily, what are you doing here?" Eliza asked, moving closer. She wondered if she could get a hug outside of the orphanage, but worried the guards would misinterpret her movement. Sister Emily would have to initiate it.

I wanted to check in on you," Sister Emily explained. "I've called a few times and thought I would stop by today. They said I could see you." Her demeanor was kind but still stiff, even without the presence of the Matron.

"Well, thank you. That's—very nice of you," Eliza said. She couldn't remember anyone caring enough to check on her before. "Do you want to take a walk?"

Sister Emily nodded and they fell into step together. "How are you adjusting to life here, Eliza?" she asked.

Eliza brushed her fingertips along the edge of a nearby holly bush and sighed. "It's all right, I guess. A lot like St. Agatha's."

"And how does Millie like it here?" Sister Emily went on.

"I don't really know," Eliza admitted. "I only see her at dinner but she doesn't speak. I think she's on a lot of medicine."

Sister Emily nodded and clasped her hands in front of her.

"How are things at the orphanage?" Eliza questioned, trying to make her voice sound bright.

"Wonderful...well, the same," Sister Emily said with a laugh. "Olivia and her husband came back and adopted Jessica last week."

"Oh, well that's...nice," Eliza said, her heart sinking a little. She tried to remember what Jessica looked like. "I'm glad that Jessica is going to a nice home." Now once Millie got out of Belle Rose, there wouldn't be anyone waiting for her.

"How is the treatment going?" Sister Emily asked carefully, winding around a large rose bush that jutted out onto the narrow path.

Eliza bit her lower lip, thinking about the terrible dream and all of the memories that had come with it. Before that night, she had felt good, confident, but now...now everything was different. She had been forced to start her progress all over again.

"Um, I'm not sure. It's fine I guess."

The pair walked in silence for the next few minutes until the small path led them back to the main square of the garden. Multiple wrought iron benches were spaced sporadically around the grass, some occupied by patients out enjoying the warm day.

Inclining her head, Eliza motioned for Sister Emily to have a seat on a nearby bench and simultaneously they sat down and sighed. A flicker of movement caught Eliza's eye and she flinched, bumping the nun.

"Are you all right, dear?" Sister Emily asked.

Speechless for a moment, Eliza followed the movement as it lazily drifted across her vision. It was just a butterfly, its bright turquoise wings glistening in the bright sunlight. "Yes, sorry, Sister Emily, I...thought I saw something else," Eliza apologized, her cheeks burning a light shade of pink. *If I can't even convince Sister Emily that I'm okay, how will I ever change Dr. Bodin's mind? What if I'm not okay?*

The nun watched as the butterfly disappeared from view and then turned to focus on the purse wedged against her side. Withdrawing a small clear box filled with tiny white pills, Sister Emily tipped the container into her palm and shook out two of them.

Eliza furrowed her brow as she watched the nun slip the pills between her lips. "Are you sick, Sister Emily?"

"Oh no," laughed Sister Emily. "These are just tic tacs. You know, little mints that make your breath smell nice. Do you want one?"

Eliza looked at the small candies. "What will they do to me?"

"Nothing, dear," Sister Emily said, shaking the small box again until one of the tic tacs jumped into her palm. "They're just nice to suck on."

Eliza reached to accept the candy when a nurse appeared, waving her hands in agitation. "Sister! Please. Do not offer any medicine. That's our job."

Sister Emily blushed. "I'm sorry, but it's just a tic tac."

The nurse's flushed face instantly cooled and she laughed. "Oh, my mistake. I'm sorry, Sister."

Sister Emily watched her go and shook her head. "Wow, everyone here is very up-tight."

Eliza glanced at the nun in surprise just as Sister Emily's hand flew to cover her mouth. Eliza giggled and held her hand out again to accept the tic tac. She popped it into her mouth, enjoying the cooling sensation enveloping her tongue. "May I have another?"

"Of course," Sister Emily smiled. "You can have all of them actually." She passed the clear box to Eliza and straightened her gray skirt.

"Thank you," Eliza smiled, accepting the box and pouring out a few more mints. "These are good."

Sister Emily nodded, warily eyeing the guards and nurses around the garden. Silence descended. Eliza didn't want to talk about St. Agatha's and she guessed that Sister Emily was too shy or nervous to ask her much about Belle Rose. Yet, even though they hadn't said much, Eliza was very glad the nun had come to visit her.

Sometime later, the towering clock above the garden tolled, marking the end of Eliza's free period. They rose to their feet and Sister Emily placed a gentle hand on Eliza's shoulder.

"It was very nice to see you, Eliza," the nun said with a smile. "I do hope you are able to get well and get away from here soon."

Eliza nodded and smiled back weakly.

"Sister...do you think it would be possible for you to visit again next week? It was really nice to see you," Eliza admitted sheepishly, looking down at the green grass.

"Of course," Sister Emily whispered, grasping Eliza's upper arm and giving it a light squeeze. "I would love to. I'll be here this time next week." With another squeeze and a small wave, she hurried through the large double doors that led back inside the institute and disappeared from sight.

Leroy appeared a few seconds later. "Ready, Miss Eliza?" he asked.

Eliza nodded and allowed him to steer her back inside. As they passed through the metal doorway, they exchanged the welcoming sunlight for the stark white walls and tile floors of the quiet hallways. Eliza smiled at the sound of her tic tacs shaking in the little box like a maraca with every step.

Leroy stopped abruptly. "And what have you got there, Miss Eliza?"

"Sister Emily gave them to me," Eliza said, shaking the little box to increase the tempo. "They're called tic tacs and they make your breath smell nice and your tongue tingle. Do you want one?"

Leroy laughed, exposing his white teeth. "Well sure. Thank you, Miss Eliza."

Eliza shook a few little mints into Leroy's palm. "I tell you, I haven't had a tic tac in years!" the guard said enthusiastically. "You need to try the orange ones, they're the best!"

"You mean they come in different colors?"

"All different colors and flavors. But, like I said, the orange are the best."

They reached Eliza's room on the third floor and Leroy unlocked the door, holding it open as Eliza walked inside.

"Thank you, Leroy. I'll see you for dinner," Eliza said.

"And thank you for sharing, Miss Eliza. Now don't go eating all those before mealtime. Don't want you to ruin your appetite."

"I won't," Eliza laughed.

Once she was alone, Eliza shook the tic tac box several more times, shaking her hips to the sound. The container was a little less than half-full and Eliza stared at it, wondering how long she would be able to make them last. As soon as she got out of Belle Rose, she was going to go to a supermarket and try every single flavor. She could only imagine how all the different colors would taste.

Her jaw dropped as a thought occurred to her. Maybe she wouldn't have to wait too long to find out.

CHAPTER

9

A LOUD KNOCK RAPPED against the door, startling Eliza. The little container she held went flying, scattering tic tacs all over the floor.

"No!" she hissed. Another knock sounded, and Eliza's heart pounded as she tried to think what to do.

"Yeah?" she called.

"Hey in there, Miss Eliza," Leroy called out as the sound of tinkling keys reached her ear. "I just wanted to let you know—"

Eliza sprang to her feet as the door opened and Leroy grinned at her as he poked his head in. "—that Dr. Bodin cancelled your meeting tomorrow. He was called away and won't be back until Thursday."

"Oh, okay, thanks Leroy!"

Leroy bowed his dark head. "No problem, I'll see you for dinner."

Eliza waved back at him and waited until Leroy had closed the door and locked it securely once more before returning to her task. Although she dreaded speaking with Dr. Bodin, she did enjoy getting out of her room. She hoped they wouldn't keep her locked up all day tomorrow.

Dropping down onto her hands and knees, Eliza began retrieving all of the tic tacs. They were difficult to locate against the white tile, and she resorted to running her fingers across the floor to find all twenty-three. The final one had scattered all the way across the room beneath the window.

Eliza straightened, clutching the precious tic tacs and gazing at the gathering of dark clouds beyond the bars. Maybe there would be a thunderstorm tonight.

A bell tinkled. Eliza glanced around the empty room, wondering if a guard was passing by, shaking his keys as Leroy often did. She looked outside again. The bright glow of the sun dipped behind a faraway cloud, blanketing the surrounding trees and green grass in a deep shadow. She pressed her face against the window, recalling the warm glow of Sister Emily's afternoon visit.

There was a flicker of movement in the garden below.

Jerking backward, Eliza threw her hand in front of her face, as if to ward off an attacker. But when her eyes were able to refocus, there was nothing and no one in the garden. Frantically she looked around, chilled by the feeling that someone was watching her. She backed up until her legs collided with the bed and she sat down, surveying the near-empty room. The white coating of the tic tacs had begun to melt in her warm grasp, leaving her hands sticky. She felt around the bed until she located the container and poured the mints inside, effectively sealing in all twenty-three.

Dismissing the odd feeling still tickling the back of her neck, Eliza scooped up her book and tried to find the page she had left off on.

As she skimmed paragraphs, the sky grew darker, the sun gone for the day. The wind began to howl, increasing its intensity until the scream seemed to shake the building.

The hair on her arms prickled to attention and Eliza couldn't ignore the rapidly changing weather any longer. She leapt off the bed and ran to the window, standing on tip-toes to peer outside. The sky was pitch black now.

Wishing her cell offered curtains or something to pull between her and what lay outside, Eliza scurried back to her bed. As she buried herself under the white sheets, a voice, barely louder than the faintest whisper, wove through her mind.

We'll see you soon, little one

The voice echoed so softly in Eliza's mind that for the briefest moment, she wondered if she had really heard it. Perhaps the wind was making her imagine things, or the mattress was groaning beneath her weight. Her heartbeat was louder than the howling wind now. Snatching her book and burying herself beneath the covers with only a bit of light peeking through, Eliza opened the book to a random page and tried to distract her mind.

She had to be imagining it.

SEVERAL HOURS LATER, Eliza was escorted to the cafeteria by Leroy. The guard was still in a jolly mood from their afternoon in the sun and had several new jokes to share with her. Eliza couldn't pay attention. Her mind was far too busy trying to nail down the best way to execute her plan.

Once they entered the large, bustling room, Eliza turned to her right and nodded to Leroy as he went to stand with the other guards against the white walls. She made her way through the section of the cafeteria where the elderly residents sat, not bothering to look up from their tables when she brushed past.

Eliza breathed in and out slowly, resisting the urge to stick her hand in her pocket to double check that the two tic tacs she had brought were still there. She didn't want to give anyone reason to be suspicious.

Plastering a smile on her lips, Eliza wove her way around the tables and dozens of nurses and patients finding their seats. She almost collided with a tall man walking in haphazard circles as he prepared to sit down. She flinched as he swayed into her and put her hands up to keep him from falling.

"Thank you, Miss Eliza," one of the guards said as he grabbed the man and set him right on his feet before settling him down into the plastic chair.

Eliza nodded and hurried toward the teen and children section in the far corner. Leann, the girl who cut, and Brianna, the bald girl, waited for her. Instead of sitting between them, Eliza turned and took the vacant seat at the table where Millie always sat. She could feel Leann's eyes on her.

A minute went by and a tall girl with spiky black hair took the seat to Eliza's right, making a loud scraping sound as she dragged the chair back. Her name was Jackie and she had trouble coping with her anger. She had been in the rec room with Eliza one day when all of a sudden she burst into a tantrum and hit another girl with a pool ball. Eliza had been careful to steer clear of her since then.

Jackie began drumming her fingers on the gray tabletop, her dark green eyes narrowed. Eliza could feel the questions and the tension in Jackie's direct stare. Before she could think what to say, Millie arrived with her nurse.

"Here we are, honey," the nurse said, pulling back the last seat at the table. "Well, Miss Eliza. What are you doing over here?"

Eliza shrugged and tried to smile innocently. "I thought I'd eat with Millie today. It's been so long since I've seen her. Is that okay?" she asked shyly.

The nurse looked around. Usually Millie and Jackie were the only ones to occupy their table and as long as she didn't start any trouble, Eliza didn't see a reason for the nurse to send her away.

"I guess that's fine. Miss Millie here could use a friendly face," the nurse said gently, giving Millie's shoulder a soft squeeze. "I'll be right back with your dinners."

Eliza watched the nurse leave and head inside the small kitchen, wondering where to start. Subtly, she turned and angled her body so that she was facing Millie. Jackie glanced up from picking at her nails but remained silent.

"Millie? Mills?" Eliza whispered.

Slowly, as if waking from a dream, Millie raised her neck and set her blind eyes in the direction of Eliza's voice. "Liza? Is that you?"

A happy smile spread across Eliza's face. "Yeah, it's me. How are you?"

Millie didn't look good. Her silver-streaked hair was washed but fell languidly in front of her face, concealing most of her features. But the one thing her hair couldn't hide was her chilling silver eyes. A shiver raced up Eliza's spine and her mind returned to that night in the swamp.

Dr. Bodin had repeatedly said that Millie was alone that night, but staring into Millie's empty eyes forced a forgotten memory back. Silver and black dancers descending gracefully from the air, surrounding Millie as they sang a bewitching melody.

Habit, and Dr. Bodin's conditioning, told Eliza to stop, to cease remembering these lies. But Dr. Bodin wasn't there, and after the strange feelings of the afternoon, the visions weren't easy to dispel.

"I'm okay, I guess." Millie took so long to reply that Eliza had forgotten she had even asked her a question. "What are you doing over here?"

Millie's words were so quiet; Eliza had to strain to hear her. She sounded like her old friend, but duller.

Eliza glanced around their table before answering, making sure none of the other guards or nurses would be close enough to overhear. "I think I have a way to get us out of here," she whispered under her breath, studying her fingernails.

Millie didn't move or react to Eliza's words in any way for several seconds. At last she leaned back in her chair, her eyes staring straight ahead. Eliza wondered if her friend had heard her.

Eliza was about to repeat herself when she felt a soft pressure gently touch her knee for the briefest moment. She glanced down and saw Millie's fingers retracting from her leg to fold neatly together in her lap. Millie had understood.

"Just hang in there, Mills," Eliza whispered as the nurse returned, balancing three trays in her arms.

"All right ladies! Looks like macaroni tonight." The nurse pushed a tray toward each girl. "Eat up!" She moved on to the next table. Eliza picked up her plastic spork and drove it into the small pile of cheesy noodles in front of her.

Back at St. Agatha's, the macaroni and cheese was often over-cooked and tended to become a gelatinous paste. Here, Eliza knew they used the kind in the blue box. She took several large bites and then slowed down, sampling some of the fruit and carrots on her tray as well.

Once the grumbling in her stomach quieted, Eliza turned back to Millie. "Sister Emily visited me today," she said, spooning another cheesy bite into her mouth.

Millie paused mid-bite and lowered her spork. "Sister Emily? Really? Why?"

Eliza shrugged and continued eating. "I don't know," she admitted. "She said that she wanted to check on us..."

Millie resumed eating, her blind eyes staring down at the table. "And what did you tell her?" she asked around a mouthful.

"That we were good," Eliza replied, her plastic utensil scraping the bottom of the Styrofoam tray with a sharp squeal. She popped the last carrot in her mouth and glanced at Millie. She had a feeling her friend wasn't asking as much as she wanted to in case someone like Jackie overheard.

A flicker of white caused Eliza to look away from her friend and she realized with a touch of anxiety that it was time for medication. A dozen or so nurses were strolling around their side of the cafeteria with small paper cups aligned on circular trays.

Eliza didn't say anything as she watched the nurse nearest them walk closer and closer, passing out the assigned pills. Pretending to examine the last of her dinner with her all-in-one utensil, Eliza used her other hand to press against her upper leg, double-checking once more that the small mints were still there.

Eliza's heart pounded faster as the nurse approached their table, but was reassured by the slight bump beneath her fingertips.

"Hello ladies," the nurse said. "So it looks like I have two for Millie," she read off, grabbing the small cup containing the two white pills and setting it down in front of Millie. "Then, one for Eliza." She sat down the cup holding the red pill. "And then two for Jackie as well," she finished, withdrawing a cup with two yellow pills and placing it in front of the other girl. "You know the drill, ladies."

Eliza pulled her cup closer, her left hand still casually resting on her pocket, and watched as Millie reached for her cup. Eliza slipped her fingers inside her pocket and withdrew the mints to the very edge of the shallow depth. With her right hand she took her red pill and placed it on her tongue, then reached for her water.

Millie had opened her mouth and was about to drop the pills into the back of her throat when Eliza threw out her hand, knocking her glass of water and the pills from Millie's hand to the floor.

In a flurry of activity, the nurse standing over them began to wave her arms up and down as if to try and stop the water from leaking out of the overturned cup while Millie moved away, scraping her chair across the tile.

"Oh my goodness, I am so sorry Millie," Eliza apologized, scooting back in her chair as she withdrew the mints from her pocket and grasped them in her sweaty palm. "Let me get them for you."

Ducking underneath the table, it took Eliza a second to find the pills against the white tile. She made a groaning sound as she bent forward in her chair to retrieve them.

"Almost...." Eliza huffed, exaggerating the effort it was taking her as she scooped up the real pills and slipped them into the top of her sock. Once they were securely hidden, Eliza grabbed the edge of the table and pulled herself up, depositing the mints in front of Millie.

Millie looked toward Eliza with a bewildered expression. Eliza wasn't clumsy and certainly didn't drop things.

"Thanks," Millie whispered, picking up the pills once more and giving them a swift blow before swallowing them with a swig of water.

"Thank you, Miss Eliza," the nurse said, her voice sweet and unsuspecting. "But let's try to be more careful next time, okay?"

Eliza nodded and smiled shyly up at the nurse. "Yes. I apologize again, Millie."

"Now, Miss Eliza, did you take your pill as well?" the nurse challenged, narrowing her gaze.

"Oh yes, sorry, I swallowed it trying to catch my water glass," Eliza explained.

The nurse looked as if she were going to say something more, but a disturbance from several tables away caught her attention. Eliza followed the nurse's gaze and saw that a new girl was throwing a temper tantrum as a nurse tried to force her to swallow a pill.

"All right, you three are good. "Ya'll finish up and then head on back to your rooms."

Eliza, Millie and Jackie nodded and watched with wide eyes as the nurse ran over to assist with the angry patient. A nurse gathered the empty and discarded trays as the guards fanned out to pair up with patients. Eliza guessed they wanted to get everyone tucked back into their rooms as quickly as possible so they could deal with the other girl without creating a chain reaction.

Leroy's tall presence loomed over Eliza and he reached out his hand to help her out of her chair. "Come on, Miss Eliza. We'll get you ready for bed now."

Eliza let Leroy pull her to her feet just as Millie's guard arrived at the table. Eliza took a step away and then glanced back over her shoulder to Millie. Her friend was staring ahead, her expression a mixture of confusion and suspicion.

Eliza smiled as she recognized that look. Whenever she was planning a prank to pull on the Matron, Millie always looked at her like that.

Hopefully tomorrow, they would have a chance to talk and Eliza would find out if her plan could work. Her smile widened as she felt Millie's scrutinizing gaze follow her and Leroy through the double doors and out of the cafeteria. A flicker of hope ignited in her chest and Eliza realized that for the first time since arriving at Belle Rose, she felt like herself again.

THE NEXT MORNING, Eliza was up, dressed, and out of bed, pacing eagerly about her small room well before Leroy came to unlock the door. Millie hopefully would have figured out by now Eliza had done something with her real medication.

Eliza heard the jangle of keys and hurried to stand before the door. She would have to calm down, have to slow her breathing, or they would know something was up.

"Morning, Miss Eliza," said Leroy as the heavy white door swung open, revealing the long white hallway beyond.

"Hey there, Leroy!" She almost skipped out the door.

"Are you hungry? I heard they're doing omelets this morning," Leroy said, pulling the door shut and locking it up once more.

"Omelets?" Eliza repeated, laughing a little at the guard's eager face. "I don't think I've ever had one before."

"What?" Leroy gasped, halting their progress down the hall. "Girl, you gonna be in for a treat then!"

Eliza smiled wider and shook her head. She didn't care what they were serving; she just wanted to see Millie.

Leroy escorted Eliza to her usual table but she turned to Millie's table instead and pulled out the same chair she had occupied last night. He opened his mouth as if to protest, then closed it and strode toward the kitchen. Eliza guessed the temptation of omelets overpowered the curiosity about her table switch.

Scooting in closer to the table, Eliza saw that Jackie was already there, twirling her spork into the Styrofoam tray listlessly. She wrinkled her nose at the sharp, squeaking sound the utensil made and waited in suspenseful silence as the majority of the other patients and nurses shuffled in. Trying to appear inconspicuous, Eliza raised her eyes and craned her neck to try and catch a glimpse of Millie every time the door opened to usher someone new inside. After twelve minutes, Millie had yet to show.

Eliza began to sweat. *If the nurses find out that Millie didn't take her pills, will she be punished?*

Dozens of thoughts raced through Eliza's mind and she debated getting up and going to look for her friend. She was slowly pushing back her chair when a nurse deposited a large tray of food in front of her.

"Sorry it took me a moment to bring your breakfast. The cooks are a little behind waiting for these eggs to fry up," she explained, handing Eliza her wrapped plastic silverware. "Enjoy, now."

"Wait!" Eliza called, biting her lower lip as she heard the desperation in her own voice.

The nurse turned around, her eyes wide.

"I was just wondering if you knew anything about Millie this morning," Eliza said, trying not to appear too curious.

"Millie?" the nurse repeated as she thought. Her eyes brightened. "Oh yes, the girl with the silver eyes? She wasn't feeling too well this morning and asked to have breakfast in her room."

Disappointment surged through Eliza and she felt her shoulders slump. "Okay, thank you," Eliza replied, looking away from the nurse and down at her plate. The bright yellow egg stared back at her, the smell of onions and peppers quickly making her stomach growl.

Millie wasn't coming to breakfast. Now Eliza would have to wait at least three hours before she would be able to talk to her, and that was only if she was feeling well enough to go to recess.

Unwrapping her spork, Eliza cut up the egg and swallowed it roughly, her throat thick. She ate in stony silence, her eyes so focused on the food in front of her that she didn't notice Jackie looking at her at first.

"I said, what is your problem?" Jackie repeated, arching her dark eyebrows.

Eliza looked up and realized Jackie had been speaking to her.

"What do you mean?" Eliza asked, putting her spork down. She thought she had been doing a good job blending in and keeping her disappointment under wraps.

"First you switch tables last night, then you drop that other girl's pills, and now you're pissed that she's not here today." Jackie didn't break eye contact. "So like I said, what's your problem?"

Eliza fumbled for words, not knowing a safe way to reply. "I don't know what you're talking about."

Jackie stared at her and Eliza watched her lips twitch. "Whatever," the other girl said at last, and returned her attention to her plate.

If I'm obvious to Jackie, does that mean other people have noticed something, too? Eliza frowned in Jackie's direction as she chewed her food. If she tried to lie, the other girl would become even more suspicious.

At last a dull buzzing signaled the end of breakfast and the nurses quickly ran about gathering the dirty trays while the patients paired back up with their guards.

Eliza watched Jackie walk away with a guard named Ernie, warring with herself whether or not she should tell the girl not to say anything. Eliza had no idea where Jackie was heading or if the girl even cared about her plans. She just hoped that she would keep her mouth shut and her nose out of their business.

"All righty, Eliza," Leroy greeted her. "Nine-thirty, guess it's time for group." He smiled, hooking his fingers through his belt loop as he waited for her to rise from her chair.

Eliza forced herself to smile and led the way to her next scheduled activity. *Just a few more hours,* she told herself as she glanced at the large clock to her left. *Just a little longer and then I can see Millie.*

Group therapy passed in much the same way as it always did. Eliza's group was made up of five other girls, all suffering from different psychological disorders. The doctor who led the session always asked the patients to share personal stories that might help explain why they ended up at Belle Rose but Eliza rarely shared.

Once, under the doctor's insistence, she had acknowledged that she had both seen and heard voices and beings, but otherwise Eliza remained mute. Today the hour and a half passed in much the same manner and Eliza exhaled with relief when the young doctor finally looked at her watch.

"And that's all the time we have for today, ladies," she said. "Maybe on Saturday we can hear from a few others. Miss—Eliza? Do you think you can share a little more about yourself with us next time?"

Eliza looked up in surprise and tucked a loose hair behind her ear. "Umm, s-sure, no problem," she stammered.

"Great," the young woman smiled, stretching her legs. "I'm sure we will all look forward to it. Have a great afternoon, ladies."

Eliza nodded to the doctor and even offered her a small smile as she grumbled under her breath. It was too bad Sister Emily wasn't coming sooner.

Eliza followed the other girls out of the small office and into the hallway where they all split according to their schedules. Eliza's weak smile grew much larger. It was eleven, which meant her free time, and Millie!

She joined up with Leroy around the corner and had to practically pinch herself to stop from running ahead. She had to remain calm and focused, otherwise she was going to blow it before she could even relay her plan.

A few minutes later, Eliza walked into the open yard, feeling Leroy melt away behind her. She had taken a few steps toward the large flower bushes where the butterflies gathered when something poked her arm.

"Hey!" Eliza exclaimed, expecting to see one of the burly guards in white. Instead she saw the familiar flash of silver as Millie's blind eyes caught the sunlight. "Mills?"

"What did you do to me?" Millie growled, her usual sweet voice harsh and gravelly.

Eliza allowed Millie to tow her around the large bushes, concealing most of their conversation from view. "What do you mean, I—ow—"

Millie's fingers were still gripping her upper arm tightly, her nails digging into her soft skin. "Last night...after dinner, I heard... what did you do?" Millie closed the distance between Eliza's face and her own.

Eliza stared at her friend. "Mills, calm down. You're supposed to be happy!"

"But what did you do?" Millie stressed.

Eliza licked her lips, feeling her spine tingle as Millie's blind silver eyes bore into her. "I have a plan to get us out," she whispered. "The other day, when Sister Emily came to see me, she brought mints, tic tacs. They look just like your pills and last night, —I switched them. That's why I knocked them out of your hand. I just wanted to see what would happen...if it would work."

Both Eliza and Millie were silent as a patient chasing a languid butterfly stumbled by. Once he rounded the corner, Eliza swallowed roughly. "So...did it work?"

Millie's expression gave nothing away.

"Mills?" Eliza asked again.

"Yes...yes it worked. For the first time I felt like, like I used to but it scared me. Usually I just go back to my room and fall asleep, but last night I dreamed *and remembered* and there were voices... memories I think, of the orphanage," Millie admitted slowly.

Eliza beamed and reached out, grabbing her friend's hands. She ignored Millie's flinch. "That's great, Mills! Don't you see? This can work! Once we stop taking those pills, we can get out of here!"

Millie shook her head, her limp hair swishing from side to side. "But how? Won't they find out?"

"Not if we keep acting like we are taking them," Eliza said happily. "Just think about it. We don't even have to pretend for that long. I asked Sister Emily to come back next week, this Tuesday! If we can just pull it off for a few more days, we'll be able to sneak out."

Millie took a step back, disentangling her hands from Eliza. "But how do you plan to get out? There are guards and nurses watching us everywhere."

"I'll figure something out. I always do, right?" Eliza said excitedly. "It'll be just like old times."

Millie was quiet for several minutes as another butterfly danced before her. Eliza watched as her friend's eyes seemed to follow the insects' movement. Could she see it?

"Old times," Millie whispered. "But where will we go?"

"Anywhere! That's what's so great! Once we get out from behind these walls we can go anywhere in the world that we want! Hop on a bus and just go until we want to stop," Eliza enthused, sparking to life as she imagined a life away from schedules and routines and counseling. "We can do it, Mills."

"But how?" Millie asked again, her voice becoming sad. "They'll catch us...they'll find me, bring me back." She frowned, a look of fear crossing her features.

Eliza waved her hand in front of her face as if to dismiss Millie's silly thoughts. "They're just guards and a few nurses, they won't even care that we're gone."

"That's not who I meant," Millie whispered. Eliza opened her mouth to ask but her friend continued, "So she's coming this Tuesday? Does she know?"

Eliza shook her head, her excitement growing. "No, of course not and we can't tell her, we can't tell anyone, okay? It'll take me a few days to work out the details but we're getting out of here, Mills!" She grabbed her friend's hands and squeezed them.

Millie nodded and glanced away, staring out over the green grass.

"Aren't you excited?" Eliza asked her, her smile fading a little.

Again, Millie nodded and turned her silver eyes back to Eliza. "Yes," was all she said.

"It'll all be fine, you'll see! Tonight I'll bring you more tic tacs and I'll come up with some way to stop taking my pill too. Just follow my lead."

"Millie? Where are you?" a deep voice called.

"I've got to go. I have a meeting with Dr. Rice. She wants to look at my eyes," Millie gasped, pulling her hands out of Eliza's.

"Okay, just be cool okay? Don't tell anyone anything about our plan," Eliza stressed.

Millie's guard called for her again. A few more steps and he would find them behind the large butterfly bush. "I got it," Millie whispered and stepped away from Eliza, using her hands to guide her as she navigated her way around the shrubs.

Eliza watched her friend leave through a gap in the branches of the bush. Millie seemed okay, better than a few weeks ago when she resembled a walking zombie, but there was still something off in her mannerisms. Her friend seemed like a shell of her former self.

Getting away from Belle Rose and the orphanage would help them both. Eliza gazed up at the blinding sun. It was going to work.

CHAPTER

10

"HERE YOU GO girls. Tonight we have chicken fingers and mashed potatoes," the nurse announced, setting all three trays down in front of the girls. "Miss Eliza, it's nice to see you here again." Her statement hung in the air, not completely accusatory but not innocent either.

Eliza shrugged and pulled her tray closer to her. "Thank you," she said, picking up a chicken finger and biting into it.

The nurse pursed her lips and turned on her heel. Eliza watched her go and then looked back down at her tray, not missing the knowing look in Jackie's eyes.

Shifting in her seat, Eliza brushed the side of her hand along her pocket, checking to make sure the two mints she carried from her room hadn't slipped out. The tiny bulge where they lay hidden greeted her search and Eliza tossed her long hair flippantly over her shoulder.

"Don't eat all of your food, Mills." Eliza whispered, picking up her spork.

Too soon the once full meal adorning their plates was reduced to crumbs and the nurses scattered about dolling out pills to each patient. Eliza had been careful to leave a small pile of mashed potatoes on her plate, hoping to hide her pill in the middle, but when she glanced over at Millie's tray she realized her friend hadn't left her with a lot of options. She couldn't hit Millie's hand again; that would be too obvious.

The nurse from earlier approached their table, a small box with different compartments in her hands. "Hey there, girls, ready?"

All three nodded and held out their hands to accept their medication. The nurse handed pills to Jackie first, then Millie, and finally Eliza.

As the nurse dropped the red pill into Eliza's palm, Eliza retrieved the two mints from her pocket with her other hand.

"All right Miss Millie, you first," the nurse instructed.

Millie slowly raised the white pills to her mouth, tilting her head toward Eliza for a signal of what to do. The nurse's dark amber eyes were glued to the pills in Millie's palm.

Eliza's brain whirred and clicked, trying desperately to come up with something, anything.

"Come on now, Miss Millie," the nurse said with an impatient sigh.

Millie's head turned in Eliza's direction as she waited for her friend to do something, but Eliza couldn't think of anything. *Maybe taking the pills just one more time won't be so bad. I'll have a backup plan tomorrow.*

Millie had raised the pills to her lips and was about to place them on her tongue when Jackie began coughing violently.

The nurse's eyes left Millie and she hurried behind Jackie, wrapping her arms underneath the girl's rib cage to perform the Heimlich maneuver.

For a second, both Eliza and Millie stared as the nurse fought to clear whatever was stuck in Jackie's throat. Then Eliza reached for her friend, the gesture intended to look like one of comfort as they made the switch, their eyes never leaving Jackie's purpling face. Eliza gave her foot a casual scratch, depositing the real pills into her sock.

With one final thrust, the nurse was able to dislodge the large piece of chicken from Jackie's windpipe. "My gracious, Miss Jackie, you gave me a fright!" the nurse exclaimed, gently rubbing the girl's back. "Are you all right now?"

Jackie nodded as her face began to fade from bright red to its usual pale shade. "Okay girls, take your pills now. We've got to get along to bed."

With a swift nod, Millie placed the mints on her tongue and swallowed, opening her mouth wide so the nurse could see they had disappeared. Eliza also tossed her pill into the back of her throat, where she caught it from continuing down. The nurse, still visibly shaken from Jackie's near-choking incident, waved her hand in acknowledgment. She looked over her shoulder for their escorts and Eliza sneezed, dislodging the pill from her throat. It struck the back of her teeth with a dull *ping*.

"Bless you," Millie whispered, offering Eliza her crumpled napkin.

"Thanks," Eliza sniffled, pressing the napkin to her nose and lips. She spit the red pill into the middle of the napkin and tossed it onto her plate where it stuck in the small pile of potatoes.

The nurse turned back. "Let's get this cleaned up," she said, and reached for their trays. As she walked away, Eliza snuck a glance at Millie and smiled. They had managed to pull off the switch after all.

Her gaze flickered over Jackie and the other girl's expression gave her pause.

Rather than her usual disapproving or uninterested countenance, Jackie was staring back at Eliza, her expression almost smug. Eliza narrowed her eyes. *Did Jackie see me swap the pills while she was choking?*

Eliza opened her lips to say something but Jackie beat her to it. "You're welcome," the older girl smirked, her green eyes lighting with humor.

"What?" Eliza gasped. She thought back to the moment before Millie was about to take the real pills. *Jackie caused a diversion.* "But..."

Jackie shook her head, silencing her. "Look, I don't know what it is that you are planning but you better start coming up with some ideas. I'll try to help you out as much as I can but...I won't get caught for you."

"Why?" Eliza mouthed, both shocked and grateful for the other girl's actions. She could see Leroy approaching.

Jackie casually scratched the back of her neck. "No one should be stuck here, locked away. If you have a chance to get out...take it." Abruptly she rose and moved to meet her guard before he reached the table.

"What just happened?" Millie whispered as she too pushed back her chair.

Eliza was quiet for a minute as she watched Jackie disappear through the doorway. "Millie, I think we've got an ally."

THE NEXT FEW days passed quietly. Millie continued to behave as if she was still on her medication and with Jackie's help, the nurses had no idea that Millie wasn't.

Eliza wasn't able to ask Millie how she was feeling now that she had been off her pills for almost a week, but noted that with each day her friend became more like her old self.

The only change that Eliza noticed from not taking her own pill was that her dreams of the swamps were returning. Seeing no harm, she decided to focus her efforts on Millie and resume taking it.

Monday afternoon arrived and with it, Eliza's last meeting with Dr. Bodin, if everything went according to plan. She smiled to herself as the doctor glanced over her file.

"Well it seems that you have been doing very well these past few weeks, Eliza," Dr. Bodin commented, laying the sheet of paper back down on his desk. "And you haven't had any more nightmares regarding these creatures?"

"No sir," Eliza said quickly. "Group has really helped me realize that it was all just an illusion."

Dr. Bodin raised his furry gray and white speckled eyebrows. "Oh really? According to Dr. Pole, you only recently started sharing in group. Why did it take you so long to open up?"

Eliza shrugged, recalling her forced sharing time during group with Dr. Pole.

"And what are your biggest fears, Eliza?" the young doctor asked, not wasting any time.

Eliza's heart sunk. She had hoped Dr. Pole would have forgotten about asking her to speak. She glanced around the small circle, finding herself the sudden focus of five sets of eyes.

"Remember Eliza, no passing this time," Dr. Pole said.

No one jumped in to save her. Eliza scooted to the edge of her seat and swallowed roughly. "I guess...losing myself."

"Losing yourself?" Dr. Pole repeated. "That's very insightful. Can you explain what you mean for everyone please?"

Eliza balled her hands into fists as they began to sweat. "I don't know. Sometimes I feel like I don't know who I am, or going to be. I don't want to lose who I am when I'm here," Eliza said honestly, hoping that would be enough to satisfy the doctor.

Dr. Pole nodded. "And why are you here? What drove those that care about you to bring you to Belle Rose?" she questioned.

Eliza scoffed, thinking about the Matron and the police, the people that supposedly cared about her. She brushed her hair out of her face and pulled her long white sleeves down over her hands, tucking the edges in between her clenched fists. "Well my friend and I, we came from an orphanage and she thought...we both thought that we found something in the swamps outside. We thought that we found fairies."

Back when she first came to Belle Rose, Eliza had been asked to share her affliction with the group, but she had never gone into detail. Even amongst the other patients, she didn't want to be considered the freak.

"But why was finding fairies so bad?" Dr. Pole asked, crossing her legs.

Eliza glanced around at the blank faces still watching her. Chances were the other girls didn't care what she was saying, so long as it wasn't them being forced to speak.

"Well, it wasn't bad at first. In fact, it was a fun way to escape the orphanage. But then...soon after, they started to change and they attacked my friend. They changed her and made her try to hurt me too," Eliza explained, beginning to feel uncomfortable.

"And why would they do that?" Dr. Pole said, a wrinkle forming on her forehead.

Eliza breathed in deeply, worried she had said too much. In all of her sessions with Dr. Bodin she told him that the fairies weren't real, that the whole thing never happened. If she wanted to maintain the little freedom that she had at Belle Rose, she would have to backtrack.

"They didn't," Eliza explained unclenching her fists.

"What do you mean?" Dr. Pole asked, confusion marring her calm features.

"There never were any fairies. We made them up...I made them up, as a way to deal with the Matron at the orphanage. She was the real one who scared me and I pretended to see them, to blame them," Eliza said.

"But why would you do that? Why create something you felt was so dangerous?" Dr. Pole said, tilting her head.

Eliza exhaled and forced herself to keep going. "Because I didn't want to see the truth. I didn't want to acknowledge that I was weak. My best friend was about to be adopted so I created the fairies to keep her at the orphanage with me. I thought that...if I made her believe too, then she wouldn't leave me. The Matron scared me but the power of the fairies quickly replaced her. But I let it go too far and my friend got out of control..." she let her voice trail off.

The group was silent as Dr. Pole made several notes on her notepad. "Thank you, Eliza, for sharing that with us. I know it must have been very difficult to open up like that."

Shaking her head, Eliza looked at Dr. Bodin, returning to the question at hand. "I'm not sure. I guess that I didn't want the other girls to judge me," she admitted.

"Oh Eliza, you mustn't fear others judgment. Everyone will always have an opinion about you and you must learn to take it with a grain of salt. As long as you are happy with yourself, that is all that matters," he said kindly, removing his glasses and polishing the lenses on his white coat's lapel.

Eliza nodded and tucked her palms underneath her thighs.

"And how do you think your friend Millie is adjusting?" he continued, sliding his thick frames back onto his nose. "What do you think she believes about the fairies?"

Eliza was taken aback. Never before in their meetings had they mentioned Millie's behavior. She had begun to wonder if it was against policy to talk about the other patients. "Um…I'm not sure sir, I don't get to talk to Millie a lot," Eliza answered.

"But you've been sitting with her at meal times haven't you? The nurses have reported that for almost a week now you have joined her and Jackie at their table," he said, considering her thoughtfully.

Eliza felt her palms begin to sweat. *He knows. We were so close!*

"Yeah but we still don't talk much. Millie is really quiet," she said, trying to appear uninterested.

"Yes, she is taking some strong medication to subdue her violent behavior that you yourself have experienced first-hand. I suppose that could be what is making her so quiet. Have you ever tried to talk to her? Ask her what she thinks?" Dr. Bodin prodded.

Eliza didn't mind lying; she had become quite good at it living in foster homes and the orphanage. But the way Dr. Bodin watched her made her skin itch. It was as if he already knew the answer and was testing her, waiting for her to say the wrong thing.

"No sir, I didn't want to get in trouble," Eliza answered, pushing back in the chair until she felt the thick cushion press against her back.

Dr. Bodin nodded and shuffled the papers on his desk. "I see. Well, thank you for your honesty, Eliza. I think that's all for today," he said dismissively, smiling without showing his teeth.

Eliza nodded and jumped out of the chair, ready to leave his warm office and get back into her cool white room, away from his searching eyes. As long as she or Millie didn't do anything crazy within the next twenty-four hours, they could still make it.

"Goodbye Eliza," the doctor called as she left.

"Goodbye," Eliza whispered.

WITH ONLY AN hour left until dinner, Eliza sat on the edge of her bed with her eyes closed, trying to envision life once she was free of the institution.

With Millie by her side, she would take them as far away as she could. They would get out of Louisiana and head north. She smiled at the thought of standing in the cold air, letting snowflakes gently kiss her face. Millie had never seen snow before; it'd be nice to show her.

Eliza's heart beat steadily in her chest as her vision continued, plunging her into a deep dream which depicted a joyous scene of the friends making snow angels and pelting one another with glistening snowballs. The sun shone so brightly in her vision that it almost blinded her, and Eliza shielded her eyes from the reflection off the crisp snow.

When she opened her eyes again, something was different, slightly off. The snowflakes still fell silently but they had more movement to them, as if someone was directing the snowfall.

Cold flakes brushed across Eliza's skin and this time, their touch made her shudder. As more snowflakes fell, their once gentle touch turned urgent and sticky, like a spider web.

Eliza tried to brush the flakes away but her fingers became entangled in the gathering strands. The strange snow was everywhere, covering her hair and dripping into her eyelashes.

Eliza's heart began to beat faster and she tried to call out to Millie for help, but the web grew longer and covered her mouth. Eliza could taste a bitter odor on her tongue as the snowy web began to accumulate over her entire body, cocooning her.

She tried to cry out but the web was slithering down her throat. Her hands clutched uselessly at her neck. She looked around frantically, but Millie had vanished with the snow.

"Help!" Eliza screamed, her plea barely louder than a whisper. "Help me!"

There is no help for you, a soft voice breathed. *You will try to escape, you will try to protect her but in the end her fate will be the same as the others. You will bring her to us and she will die as she must.*

Eliza stopped struggling. That voice, she knew that voice, would never be able to forget it. Once again the fairies had somehow reached her, able to infiltrate her mind. She tried to shake herself awake, but the dream held fast.

No matter where you try to run, you will always come back.

The suffocating web was too much. Soon Eliza would be trapped forever inside her mind by the fairies' magic.

With a loud, guttural scream, she reached up and slid her fingers underneath the sticky substance, tearing it with all her might. She heard the fairies laughing at her, their husky voices a terrifying melody that tried to pull her back under their control. With another wild cry, Eliza broke free from her prison and exploded from the dream.

The stark, white walls of her room surrounded her, the firm mattress underneath her back once more. She sighed in relief, touching her neck as her breathing steadied. She shuddered, still able to imagine the spider web spinning down her throat.

The door slammed open and Eliza screamed.

"Eliza! Eliza, are you all right?" Leroy bellowed, barreling in.

"Yes, I'm fine, just fine! What's wrong?" He couldn't know what she had been dreaming.

"You were screaming at the top of your lungs," Leroy panted, staring at her.

Eliza frowned. He must have come running from the staff room down the hall. *If he heard me in the staff room, someone else might have to. What if Dr. Bodin heard? Will he put me on lockdown?*

What's wrong, Eliza? Who hurt you?" Leroy asked, coming closer to where she sat on the bed.

Several other nurses and guards entered her room and Eliza closed her eyes as defeat washed over her. There was no way Dr. Bodin wouldn't hear about this. She had to say something and fast.

"No one, Leroy...it was just a bad dream," Eliza explained, crossing her arms over her chest and hunching her shoulders, trying to make herself smaller. "I didn't know I was yelling. I'm sorry."

Leroy shook his dark head and put his hands on his hips. "That weren't no yelling, Miss Eliza. That was a blood-curdling scream at the top of your lungs. I thought we'd run in and find someone stabbing you to death."

Eliza shrugged. "Sorry, I'm fine," she mumbled.

"What were you dreaming about?" Leroy asked her. Eliza raised her eyes and felt bad; the guard looked scared.

She shrugged again and looked back down at the floor. "I don't remember," she whispered.

Eliza heard Leroy exhale loudly, signaling that he didn't believe her. She glanced around at the small staff, seeing several eye rolls and pursed lips. She would rather they think her a liar than know what terrifying visions and voices her mind could conjure. If she was truthful, she would be locked away forever.

Eliza scooted forward on her bed and looked squarely at Leroy. She had to make him think that she was fine, convince him and herself that what just happened had been nothing more than a dream. "Um, can I take a short walk around the halls before dinner? I think I've been in this room for too long today."

Leroy shook his head again and gestured to the still open door. "Come on then."

Everyone in the room began to file out, mumbling under their breath. Eliza felt her face turn red but did her best to ignore them. Soon they wouldn't matter, no one there would matter.

She stepped into the hallway with no destination in mind. She just needed to get away from the quiet. She heard Leroy lock her door before following, his large presence unusually close.

Not bothering to look over her shoulder, Eliza sighed. "You don't have to follow me you know," she said, trying to keep the annoyance out of her tone.

Leroy laughed and adjusted his belt that carried the key ring. "Yeah right, after an episode like that you think you can just walk around by yourself. You know better than that, Miss Eliza."

She wasn't sorry to have company, but found his close presence an annoying reminder she had messed up again. She had to be more careful. Tomorrow was Tuesday, and she still had planning to do. She needed to map out their escape route.

"Where are you going, Miss Eliza?" Leroy asked as she turned down a new hallway.

"I'm just exploring," Eliza laughed. "Sometimes it feels good to walk."

"It does," agreed Leroy.

For the next half hour the guard followed her meanderings through the hallways, silent and apparently lost in his own thoughts. Eliza climbed stairs, turned corners and wandered down unfamiliar hallways, passing offices decorated with fake plants, a game room, supply closets and finally the cafeteria. Eliza slowed her steps as they approached the large doors. The sounds of the nursing staff setting the tables up could be heard on the other side.

Eliza sighed. She had yet to find the front door.

"Okay, Miss Eliza, let's head on inside. I heard that we got gumbo tonight," Leroy said, rubbing his large gut.

There wasn't anything else Eliza could do but nod and give up her search. It was beginning to look like they would just have to wing it and hope for the best tomorrow. Once they found a way outside, Sister Emily was their ride to freedom.

Taking a step toward the tall doors, Eliza put her hand on the metal handle and was about to pull it open when loud shouts from behind them startled her.

"Roy! Leroy, come quickly! One of the patients!" another guard yelled as he ran by and disappeared around the corner leading to vacant offices.

Eliza glanced back at Leroy.

"Not to worry, Miss Eliza. You go on in there and enjoy your dinner. I'll see you later," the guard's deep voice boomed as he jogged away from her in the same direction the other guard had left.

She stared down the hallway, torn. Part of her wanted to keep exploring and find the exit. No one inside the cafeteria had seen her yet and Leroy was preoccupied.

If she got caught it could hurt her chances tomorrow.

But if she didn't, tomorrow could be a total fail anyway.

Biting her lower lip, Eliza gripped the handle, her palm sweating. It was now or never. Dinner would be starting soon and the nurses escorting other patients down would see her and start asking questions.

Eliza let go of the handle, turned, and ran down the same hallway Leroy had disappeared into. She could hide in one of the offices and wait out the dinner rush.

The hallway contained six offices, three on either side. Choosing the middle on the left at random, Eliza ducked inside and closed the door, leaving it slightly ajar in case it locked from the inside. She hid behind the large desk, sitting on the floor for extra precaution.

Not even a minute later, Eliza heard a loud shout and the sounds of multiple people nearby. She ducked lower and looked around the room, confused as to where the noises came from. There was a door in the back left corner, presumably a closet.

Raising herself back onto her knees, Eliza carefully crept across the room and pressed her ear to the white wood. Voices drifted through.

"Hold him down! Secure his legs! I've got him!"

Eliza frowned. It sounded as if several guards were trying to subdue a patient inside the closet, but that didn't make sense.

Wrapping her palm around the brass handle, Eliza gently turned it to the right and gasped when it opened easily. She expected to see a dark broom cupboard with a few coat hangers staring back at her, but was greeted by a very different sight.

A bright white room gleamed before her, the shiny tiled floor similar to the one lining the hallways. The room was large and airy, with a large desk adorned by a beautiful bouquet of flowers.

Eliza pushed the door open a little wider and peered around the edge. A woman stood behind the desk, watching as three guards pinned down an elderly male patient. The tile around him was smeared with bright red blood.

"Come on, let's get him up," one of the guards ordered and Eliza recognized Leroy's voice.

She watched as the three guards helped the man to his feet. When they turned him around, Eliza saw he had a nasty cut just above his eyebrow. Blood still dripped down his face and onto the floor. She shivered, involuntarily remembering the scene back at the orphanage, when Millie had been under the fairies' spell and hurt Lacey.

Eliza studied the room, intent on forgetting that incident. Several of the tiles were orange rather than white, but it wasn't blood staining them. She craned her neck to the right and saw a large floor-to-ceiling window. The last of the sun's rays were sparkling through the glass, transforming the tiles with a soft golden glow.

Through the window was a sea of black, filled with cars. The truth hit her suddenly. She had found it. She had found the front door! This was the lobby!

Eliza's heart began to hammer in her chest. *I did it! I found the way out!*

The woman behind the desk walked to a door on the other side of the hall, withdrew a yellow bucket and mop and wheeled it over to the smeared blood in front of the glass doors. Eliza noted they didn't automatically open. Like every other door at Belle Rose, it required a key.

Eliza slowly withdrew back into the office and shut the door. She had solved one problem, only to discover another.

"What are you doing in here?" a stern voice called out.

Eliza's heart leapt into her throat as her mind froze. What possible reason could she give to explain her unsupervised detour?

Dozens of thoughts tried to take shape but they all dissolved as the fear of being put in lock-down crippled her. She spun, flinging a fist out in desperation. Her punch connected with a light thud, not doing any damage as despair crushed her strength. She looked grimly at the person who had caught her.

"Jackie! You scared me half to death! What are you doing in here?" Eliza demanded.

Jackie smiled and tossed her short, jagged hair out of her eyes. "I could ask you the same question."

She was smiling, but Eliza's stomach twisted. This was it, the part where Jackie turned on her and told Dr. Bodin what she was up to. Eliza tried to form a reply but her tongue seemed to be swollen.

The other girl seemed to be waiting for Eliza to say something. When she didn't, Jackie huffed and put her hands on her hips. "Oh relax, would you? I was on my way to dinner when I heard a noise. I came to check it out and found you doing the same...right?" Jackie raised her eyebrows knowingly, giving Eliza the chance to save herself.

"Yes...there was a banging sound. I was just checking to see if anyone was hurt," Eliza said slowly, and Jackie nodded encouragingly.

Maybe the other girl wasn't planning on ratting her out after all.

"So what did you find?" Jackie asked, smirking a little.

Eliza hesitated. *If I tell Jackie and the nurses ask her about us tomorrow after we escape, she might tell.*

She was contemplating how much to explain when Jackie shrugged and spun on her heel.

"You still don't trust me, huh? Whatever, I'm going to eat." Jackie said.

If she does tell, we will be long gone.

"Wait!" Eliza called, knowing she was being unfair to the girl, who had proven herself only to be helpful to them.

Jackie paused, her hand on the door frame. "What?"

Eliza closed the short distance between them and stopped right behind Jackie, her hands fluttering uselessly in front of her. "I was...I was looking for a way out. And I found...the front door."

Jackie smiled, her green eyes alert. "Ah, so you found it! Pretty clever right? Never would have thought to look for the front door in the back of an office."

"How'd you know where it was? I've been here for weeks and never saw it once."

Jackie shrugged. "I remember when my parents dropped me off. Not everyone committed is brought in all drugged up," she said.

Eliza shivered as she thought back to the night she chased after Millie. She had been trying to save her friend then, but this time she would succeed.

"So, are you going to need me tonight?" Jackie asked as she motioned for Eliza to exit the office.

Eliza checked it was safe before stepping across the threshold and out into the white hallway. When the coast was clear, both she and Jackie started up a casual pace in the direction of the cafeteria.

"What do you mean?" Eliza asked, keeping her voice light in case anyone was nearby.

"You know...hopefully I won't choke on my food tonight," Jackie said, playing along.

Eliza gasped. She had been so eager to get out of her room after her dream that she had forgotten to grab the mints. "Oh no! I don't have them! I have to go back to my room!" Eliza cried, darting ahead.

"Whoa, slow down, girl," Jackie whispered, pulling Eliza back by her arm. "Just think this through first. What are you going to say? 'Hey, I need to go get something,' and then you just happen to knock Millie's pills out of her hand again? The nurses aren't smart but they're not that dumb."

"So what am I going to do? Millie can't take her pills. We're going to leave tomorrow!" Eliza banged her fist against the concrete wall.

"Will it really be so bad if she takes them one last time?" Jackie asked quietly as she pulled open the doors to the cafeteria.

"Yes!" Eliza whispered back furiously. "I've just got her weaned off of their medicine, if she takes the pills again then who knows the state she'll be in tomorrow."

The pair reached their table and sat down. Millie had yet to arrive.

"Have you been paying attention to her lately?" Jackie continued, keeping her voice low. "Your friend is already in a weird state."

Eliza frowned. What was Jackie talking about? Millie was fine; better than fine, she was acting like her old self again. Obviously she had to act quiet and restrained in front of the staff, but during the few times they had found some privacy, in the halls or out in the garden, Millie was bright and alert and ready to leave Belle Rose behind.

"What do you mean?" Eliza scoffed, ready to deny whatever silly notion Jackie thought.

"This whole week Millie's been...I don't know, agitated, I guess."

"Agitated how?" Eliza questioned, her hands gripping the table.

Jackie sighed and ran her fingers through her short hair. "How can you not see it? Every time someone walks by she flinches like she's about to be hit. And then sometimes she just stares off into space and hums that song over and over again."

"What?" Eliza demanded. She had never seen Millie act that way.

Jackie put up her hands as if in surrender. "All I'm saying is be careful. I don't know what that girl was like before she got here but if she's like this without her meds...I wouldn't want to be alone with her," Jackie finished, and looked away to signal she was done talking.

Just then Eliza caught sight of Millie slipping into the cafeteria, her guard at her side.

Jackie was crazy, a pathological liar. Eliza wasn't going to listen to her. Millie was her friend, not Jackie's. If there was something wrong with Millie then Eliza would know.

"Hey Mills," Eliza greeted a little too cheerfully as her friend sat down.

Jackie cocked her head to the side and raised her eyebrows. Eliza shook her head and balanced her head on her right fist, effectively blocking Jackie from her sightline.

"So how was your day?" Eliza asked, her eyes flickering all over her friend, trying to spot anything abnormal.

"Fine I guess," Millie answered, turning her head in the direction of Eliza's voice. "Are we still doing this?" she went on, dropping her voice lower.

"Ahh." Eliza paused, her brain frantically trying to think of a solution. She sighed. "Umm, Mills I didn't, I don't have them." Sparing a quick glance at Jackie, Eliza swallowed the guilt building thick in her throat. "Maybe we'll just have to take the real ones tonight and then that's it, no more ever again."

"No!" Millie growled. "I can't take them. They take them away. I need to know where they are!"

Eliza leaned away from Millie, caught off guard. "I know I usually take them away but I don't have any mints tonight. I'm sorry."

"No," Millie said, her pale eyes never leaving Eliza's face.

Eliza didn't know what to do. "Millie, please."

"Hey, Millie, need a napkin? I think they're serving gumbo tonight so it's going to be messy," Jackie laughed lightly, placing a folded napkin in front of Millie. "You'll need one too." Jackie set down another napkin in front of Eliza.

"Thanks," Eliza said, raising her eyebrows.

The other girl smiled and tugged on her ear quickly, pretending to brush her fingers through her short hair again.

Eliza's eyes widened as she understood. Jackie had pills, maybe not tic tacs but she had a plan to help them through tonight.

Reaching out, Eliza put her palm flat on her napkin but didn't notice anything hidden beneath the several layers. She pulled hers closer and let it fall on her lap. She moved to help Millie, and her thumb grazed two small bumps beneath the napkin.

Careful to not let the hidden pills fall as she transferred the napkin from the table to her friend's lap, Eliza tucked the napkin onto Millie's thighs, smiling brightly.

"There's your napkin, Millie. Just be careful you don't let it fall to the floor, wouldn't want to *waste it*," Eliza stressed.

Millie didn't reply but Eliza felt her cool hand slide over the napkin, securing it and the hidden pills in place. Eliza leaned away, noting how quickly her friend was relaxing now that they had a plan.

"Have you ever had tic tacs before?" Eliza asked Jackie, trying to phrase her question innocently.

"Nope, but I did a lot of self-medicating before I came here," she said with a wide smile, fluttering her lashes back at Eliza.

Eliza almost choked. "Oh?" Eliza replied, arching her eyebrows. *What did she give Millie?!*

"Mostly stuff for headaches and temperament but my favorite was the stuff for anxiety," Jackie went on smoothly. "It was great, the light yellow pills just calmed me down and allowed me to think straight for a few hours...harmless." She smiled again.

Eliza exhaled loudly. If the pills Jackie gave her were anti-anxiety then Millie should be fine. At least they would be better than whatever were in her other ones, the ones that turned her into a zombie. But they weren't white. Hopefully the nurse wouldn't notice.

"What are you ladies talking about over here?" a nurse asked as she delivered the three trays of food to their table.

"Nothing really," Jackie answered. "Just life before we came here." She picked up her spork and dove straight into the dark red gumbo.

"Oh yeah? Any fun stories?" the nurse asked.

"Nope...nothing beats this place for fun," Jackie said, her tone heavy with sarcasm.

"Watch it, Miss Jackie," the nurse warned as she moved away.

"That was rude," Eliza hissed as she picked up her spork.

"Did you want her to stand there all night?"

The trio sat in silence for several minutes, enjoying the spicy gumbo as it traveled over their tongues. Eliza snuck glances at her friend, but nothing jumped out at her as out of the ordinary. It didn't matter if Millie did act strange; tomorrow they would be free to act as they wanted. She twirled her spork in the remaining gumbo liquid. "So, Mills, are you excited to see Sister Emily tomorrow?"

"Yes," Millie smiled, her blind eyes shining. "It'll be good to see them again."

"Well Mills, only Sister Emily is coming," Eliza clarified, glancing at her friend.

"I know," Millie whispered and went back to eating her dinner.

Eliza frowned, but the nurse was headed their way, a tray of pills in her hand. Eliza pushed her discarded tray away from her and waited for her dosage. One last time.

CHAPTER

11

"THERE THEY ARE, Sister. It was so nice to see you again," the nurse said as she gestured to the green grass where both Eliza and Millie were seated in the garden.

Hearing the nurse's voice, Eliza glanced up and saw Sister Emily, clothed in her usual soft gray dress. The nurse waved and left them to their visit.

"Sister Emily!" Eliza shouted, jumping to her feet. "You came!" She raced toward the nun and was about to throw her arms around her when she remembered the nun's rigidity and decorum. Eliza slowed and reached for a handshake instead.

Sister Emily smiled and wrapped her warm hand around Eliza's. "Of course I came," the nun laughed. "I told you I would, didn't I?"

Eliza shrugged and let her hand fall away from the nun's as she pointed to where Millie sat, waiting for them. "Do you want to join us? We wanted to have a picnic but we're not permitted to have food outside," Eliza explained as she and Sister Emily wandered over to Millie.

"Sure, it's nice to get off my feet," Sister Emily said with a smile, squatting down low and then sitting back, using her hands to steady her. "Hello Millie, how are you?"

Millie turned her head in the direction of Sister Emily's voice. "Hello, Sister Emily," she whispered.

"I wasn't able to see you last time I was here. How do you like it here?" the nun asked.

Millie shrugged and reached out to run her palm along the soft grass. Slowly she separated out a blade of grass from the rest and pulled on it until the little white root broke free from underground. "It's okay," Millie said at last.

Sister Emily looked toward Eliza. "And are you still doing okay?"

Eliza smiled brightly, trying to make up for Millie's lack of excitement with her own. "Yes," she answered happily. "I even made another friend!"

"Well that's wonderful, Eliza," Sister Emily said, her shoulders relaxing. "All of the girls still talk about you at the orphanage."

"Really? That's nice. Has anyone else been adopted since last week?" Eliza continued. She was glad to see Sister Emily but couldn't wait for the small talk to be over with.

"Yes! On Friday Lacey was adopted by a nice family," Sister Emily said cheerfully, then glanced at Millie and faltered.

Eliza's heart fluttered when she heard Lacey's name and she turned to look at Millie as well. If Millie remembered hurting Lacey she gave no indication of it. Her friend continued to methodically separate and pull out individual blades of grass.

Eliza watched her, remembering the day before the craziness began, when they had wanted nothing more than to survive their time with the Matron. Eliza had been on the verge of telling Millie her escape plan while her friend had slowly pulled the grass out piece by piece, just like now.

She chuckled and stretched out her legs, wanting to draw Sister Emily's attention away from Millie. "That's wonderful! Do they have any other kids?" she asked.

"Two. A boy and a girl, and a dog," the nun answered, her smile genuine. "I think she's more excited to have the dog than siblings actually."

Eliza and Sister Emily laughed, easing the tension Lacey's name had created. Eliza could tell that the nun was curious about Millie and wanted to ask her more questions, but Millie's lack of interest in their visitor was clear.

"So how long can you stay?" Eliza asked, already knowing the answer. Visitors were only allowed in the hour after lunch. She wasn't interested in Sister Emily's answer; she just needed to start steering the conversation in the right direction.

"Only until about one-thirty unfortunately," Sister Emily said, glancing down at her watch. "Sister Mary needs the car to bring several of the girls to the doctor for their physicals later this afternoon."

Eliza smiled, glad the Sister had mentioned the car. "Did Matron Criggs get a new van yet? Or do you still have to drive that awful station wagon?"

Sister Emily hung her head and raised her hand to block her face. "Shh, not so loud or people will know I drove that horrid thing here."

"Does it still reek of old socks?" Eliza laughed wildly, waving her hand in front of her nose. "Gosh, the one time I rode in it I gagged the whole way."

"Yes! We've tried hundreds of air fresheners but nothing works," laughed Sister Emily.

"Did the nurses ask you to park a mile away so that it wouldn't smear the pretty front entrance?" Eliza giggled. She watched the nun's face closely.

"No thank goodness, I'm not sure if I would be able to take that humiliation," Sister Emily answered. "No, there were still several spots in the visitor's lot so I got a spot right up front. They'll probably make an announcement any moment though, once they realize just how ugly the car is, and ask me to leave."

"Oh no, that'd be awful," Eliza sympathized as she pictured what she had seen of the parking lot.

The close proximity was a blessing and a curse. It would make it easy to quickly cross the lot and reach the car, but on the other hand, the closer it was to the building, the closer it was to the cameras and the check-in desk.

Eliza brushed her hair out of her eyes and was asking Sister Emily more questions about the orphanage when Millie suddenly twisted her neck to look over her shoulder.

The sharp movement made Eliza stop mid-sentence.

"They're here," Millie whispered. "I need to get away, we need to leave. It's almost time, time, time for me. Back to the...under the tree... swamp and dark...flowers and blood to find..." Her blind eyes stared up at the bright blue sky.

"Mills, are you okay?" Eliza asked, reaching out her hand to steady her friend.

Millie flinched violently at the unexpected contact and her head swiveled forward at a dangerous angle.

Sister Emily looked from one girl to the other and slowly rose to her feet. "You know, I think I should be going actually. I don't want to make Sister Mary late for the doctor," she explained, fear evident in her light brown eyes.

Eliza watched the scared nun back away from Millie and felt panic. It wasn't time yet! Millie was supposed to leave and hide in the bathroom and wait for Eliza to come get her! *What are you doing Millie? You're going to ruin the entire plan!*

"Millie? Mills, it's okay. Remember we are visiting with Sister Emily? Remember we had that planned for today?" Eliza implored. If the nurses saw her acting like this, they would bring her back to her room and Eliza would never be able to get her out in time.

Millie continued to mutter to herself and stare at a fixed point in the sky, Eliza's words unable to reach her.

"Should I get someone to help?" Sister Emily asked, looking around the garden for a nearby nurse. Eliza's breath caught as the nun waved one of the guards over.

Leaning in close to Millie's ear, Eliza whispered instructions almost violently. "Listen Mills, you do exactly as I say and wait for me in the bathroom. I'll be right there to get you and then we have to leave. Snatch the keys and go before Sister Emily leaves. Do you hear me?"

Millie continued mumbling jumbled words and singing a strange melody Eliza couldn't place.

"Is everything all right?" the young guard asked, walking up to the trio. Eliza had seen him around but wasn't sure of his name.

"Um, I think Millie needs some help, right Eliza? She just started muttering and singing nonsense," Sister Emily told the guard.

Eliza jumped in, hoping to save the situation before it became irreversible. "Oh no, I think it's just the heat getting to her. Normally we don't sit out in the sun for this long and it's really hot today. I think she just needs to cool down and wash her face. Can I take her to the bathroom?"

The guard shook his head. "You finish your visit with your guest. I can escort her to the restroom."

"I'm actually on my way out now," Sister Emily said, gathering her purse close to her body.

"Well, I'll walk out with you...or at least go as far as I can," Eliza said and smiled, helping Millie to her feet. She held out Millie's hand to the guard and stepped away, watching as the pair walked slowly back inside the cool building. Hopefully they would reach the bathroom fast.

Aware of Sister Emily's anxiety to get out of Belle Rose, Eliza, along with another guard, walked back inside with the nun beside her.

From her exploration yesterday, Eliza knew that the bathroom was just down the hall, a quick throw from the empty offices that led to the front door. Somehow she would need to stall Sister Emily at the check-in desk long enough for her and Millie to regroup and reach the car before she left.

As the small group navigated through the white halls, the guard introduced himself as Owen.

"Well hello," Sister Emily smiled over her shoulder. "Have you worked here long?"

Eliza stepped back so that Owen could walk alongside Sister Emily and introduce himself. She looked around desperately, needing a way to stall. She could pretend to get hurt, or cause a scene.

Nothing realistic was coming to mind and Eliza groaned inwardly. *Why didn't Millie wait for the signal?*

She glanced back up at Sister Emily and Owen, who were still deep in conversation. Eliza could see that the nun's cheeks were pink as Owen flirted with her. *Good, maybe Sister Emily has her own reason to linger.* The nurse's footsteps had slowed, and her leather brown satchel bounced against her leg, gaping open.

Sitting in plain view were the car keys.

A ray of hope blossomed as her mind took off while they rounded the last corner. Down one more hallway and through the office "closet" waited the front door. Eliza hoped Millie hadn't forgotten what she told her and wandered off.

As predicted, Owen turned around and raised his hand. "All right Eliza, this is as far as patients are allowed. You can say goodbye to Miss Emily now, okay?"

Eliza stepped toward Sister Emily, giving the nun a large smile. "Thank you so much for coming, Sister Emily. I'm sorry that we weren't able to visit for very long," Eliza told her sweetly.

Sister Emily smiled back. "Yes, maybe next time we will have more time."

"Do you know when you'll be able to return?" Eliza asked, taking another step closer.

Sister Emily looked uncomfortable for a moment, no doubt remembering how strangely Millie had acted. Eliza guessed the gentle nun never wanted to come back.

"Um, I'll have to see. I told Matron Criggs I had some personal errands to attend to, but I'm not sure I'll be able to use that excuse again for a while," Sister Emily admitted.

"Don't worry, we'll see one another soon," Eliza replied, trying to comfort the young woman. "Is it okay if I give you a hug goodbye?"

Eliza watched as Sister Emily's spine stiffened. Even away from the Matron, Sister Emily was conscious of her rules.

"Ah," Sister Emily paused, glancing up at Owen. "I think that'll be fine."

Eliza closed the last few feet separating them and wrapped her arms around the nun's petite waist. With her left hand, Eliza carefully reached into the nun's purse and felt the cool metal keys.

Wrapping the keys tightly in her closed fist, Eliza squeezed the nun with her upper arms and then let go, withdrawing both hands away from Sister Emily's body and clutching them together in front of her.

"Thank you so much for coming to visit me again," Eliza said happily as she began to walk backward. "Enjoy the rest of your day!"

"Goodbye, Eliza. Say goodbye to Millie for me," Sister Emily called, waving back.

"Oh I will!" Eliza laughed and, with a nod to Owen, turned back down the hallway they had just come from. As soon as she was out of sight, she took off at a sprint. Millie had to be there; this was their chance! Eliza squeezed the keys for reassurance. The tiny metal teeth bit into her soft skin, the pain a good reminder to run faster.

Please, please let Millie still be there.

For two minutes she ran, but it felt like a century. At last the restroom sign gleamed like a beacon before her. Outside, Millie's guard slouched against the wall, staring at his sneakers. Eliza exhaled with relief; Millie was still inside.

She moved toward the bathroom, then remembered the keys. She had to stash them somewhere obvious enough for Sister Emily to find. Carefully backtracking, Eliza slipped down the hallway that led back out to the gardens, then realized she couldn't get outside undetected. She slowed, bouncing the keys in her palm as she considered what options she had.

She was running out of time. She glanced up and down the hall, wound up her arm and pitched the keys low, as if she were playing baseball. The keys went halfway down the hallway before they hit the floor and slid, bouncing to a stop against the double doors leading to the garden.

It wouldn't take long for Sister Emily or Owen to find them. Eliza raced back to the bathroom, slowing her pace as she neared the guard.

"Hey, is Millie still in there?" Eliza called, her voice shaking slightly. Hopefully he hadn't heard the quiver.

The guard looked up and adjusted his posture. "Yes, she's been in there a long time. I was just about to check on her," he said.

"That's okay, I can do it," Eliza offered. She pushed open the door and paused. "What's your name?"

"Jason," he said, smiling back at her.

"Jason...my guess was way off," Eliza giggled and let the door swing shut behind her. "Mills?" she whispered, surprised to find the sink area empty. She pushed open the first stall and found nothing but the toilet.

"I'm here," a soft voice whispered at the far end of the bathroom.

Eliza withdrew her head from the first stall and looked around. Millie was standing at the very end, her silver eyes piercing under the fluorescent lights. "Hey," she said, crossing the bathroom in three large strides. "Are you ready to get out of here?"

"Yes," Millie replied, her face relaying no emotion.

"Okay, give me three minutes to distract Jason and then you come out," Eliza said. She walked over to the sink and splashed cold water on her face. This was it.

Eliza glanced up at Millie in the mirror and watched as her friend slowly turned her head in Eliza's direction, a thin smile stretching across her lips. Involuntarily Eliza shivered, glanced back at her own reflection and jumped.

For a flicker of a second, her own eyes had been bleached silver, her mouth carved into a sadistic smile. "Whoa," Eliza breathed, letting go of the counter and bringing her hands to her face. She waited. Nothing but her usual amber eyes stared back.

Eliza heard Millie call Jason's name, and when she turned her friend was nowhere to be found. "Mills?" she asked as the bathroom door swung open and Jason's head poked in.

"Hey, is everything okay? Do you ladies need help?" Jason asked, slowly sliding into the bathroom foyer as the door swung shut. "Where's Millie?"

"I'm not sure...I was looking in the mirror and then when I looked back she was gone," Eliza said truthfully.

Jason took several more steps into the bathroom, his hands on his belt, Millie slid out of the first stall as he passed it. Eliza cocked her head and noticed Millie was clutching something large that resembled a shield.

"Millie?" Eliza whispered, shocked.

Jason had turned his head in Millie's direction as the girl swung the porcelain toilet cover with a shrill yell, driving it with unbelievable strength into his back. The guard fell to his knees with a pained cry. Eliza took a step forward, lamely reaching her hands out as if she could have caught him.

Millie wasn't finished.

Gritting her teeth, Eliza's eyes widened and her mouth froze open in a silent scream as Millie slammed the porcelain downward, colliding with Jason's head in a terrifying crack. The young guard crumpled, a thin rivulet of blood running from the back of his head onto the white tile.

Eliza's jaw dropped and the scream she was trying to release began to choke her.

Millie tossed the cover to the floor where it shattered and bounced, scattering porcelain shards and blood in a wide arc. She slowly lifted her head to look at Eliza. "We need to go," Millie said softly, again devoid of emotion.

Eliza stared, silently, numbly, still unable to form a coherent syllable. Her tongue felt swollen, massive inside her mouth as she stared at her friend and the bloodied guard at her feet. Finally,

Eliza forced the words from her throat. "Millie, what...what did you do?"

Millie looked up from the floor and then cocked her head at Eliza's question. "What do you mean?"

Eliza stuttered as a chill spread up her spine. For the second time that day her mind jumped back and it was Lacey lying on the cold bathroom tile, her long blonde curls stained deep maroon from the spreading blood beneath her. But Lacey had woken up, had been adopted. Jason wasn't going to be that lucky.

Taking a cautious step toward Jason's limp body, Eliza didn't take her eyes off Millie. This was bad, so bad! "Why did you hit him?" she whispered.

"We have to go. We have to get away from them," Millie said, her voice void of all emotion or infliction.

Eliza moved numbly to the door. Millie was right. If she didn't get Millie away now, her friend would be locked up for life. They both would. They weren't just running away now; they were responsible for murder. She pushed the door open and peered out. The coast was clear.

Millie hadn't meant to do it. She couldn't have. Eliza shook her head. "Come on," she ordered. "We have to get to the car before Sister Emily does. She might have already found the keys." Keys. They would need keys to get out the front door. She looked back at Jason's body. "Mills, we need to get his key out."

Millie looked at Eliza and let her hands fall to her side, making no move toward the guard's body.

"Back up, I'll get it," Eliza instructed, gently touching Millie's hip to signal she should step back. Taking a deep breath, she bent down and began tugging on Jason's belt.

The keys rattled and shook with her efforts, but they were stuck underneath his weight. Eliza grunted as she tried to lift his back and free the keys. He was too heavy. "Come on, let go," she huffed through gritted teeth. Closing her eyes, she tried to roll him over without success. A slight jingle made her open her eyes.

Millie was standing over Jason's head, the bloodied keys sitting in her palm quietly like a trained sparrow. "Mills, how did you get those?"

Millie remained silent, her blind eyes staring unwavering at the keys as the blood began to pool in her palm. Spreading across her hand, the dark crimson color spilled over and raced down her forearm, soaking her white sleeve in seconds.

Eliza's stomach flipped at the gruesome sight and the smell of rust and copper overwhelmed her. Straightening from her crouch, Eliza grabbed the keys Millie offered her. The tiny jagged teeth bit into her skin, the cool metal slippery.

"Come on," Eliza grimaced, wiping her palm on her white pants. She grabbed Millie and together they slipped out into the deserted hallway.

Millie's hand was wet against Eliza's palm and her friend remained silent as they moved rapidly, careful not to press their bodies against the plaster walls until the office was in sight.

"Come on, Mills, we're almost there," Eliza said breathlessly. She was tugging her across the office threshold when the door leading to the lobby opened.

"I just don't understand it. I put them in my purse after I got here," floated Sister Emily's voice through the room, freezing the girls in place.

Eliza backtracked and pressed both her and Millie against the outside wall. She had to think fast. They would be seen in seconds! "Hurry! In here!" she hissed, shoving Millie into the last office. Like the other one, it was sparsely decorated with only two chairs and a desk. "Under the desk, go!"

With a hard shove, Eliza pushed Millie in the direction of the desk with a grunt just as she heard Sister Emily and Owen's feet in the hallway. With no time to wedge herself in, Eliza quickly jumped behind the door.

"Well we can backtrack to the courtyard and see if anyone has found them," Owen was saying.

Eliza shrunk lower and aligned herself just behind the finger-width crack. Hopefully no one else had stumbled upon the keys... or Jason's body.

"Yes, I think that would be the best idea," Sister Emily said.

A moment later, the couple disappeared around the corner, their soft voices lost. Not wasting any time, Eliza skirted the desk and grabbed Millie's upper arm. "We have to hurry!" she whispered.

The two girls bolted out of the office and into the center one. Millie turned and started to shut the door behind them.

"No! Leave it, if or they'll know someone was here," Eliza said.

Sliding her fingers along the wood, Millie slowly crossed the room to where Eliza stood. Light red streaks of blood glared against the white paint. *Nothing we can do about that,* Eliza decided, and pulled the interior door open.

The lobby was quiet. A young secretary was seated behind the desk, the panels coming up to just under her chin. If they crouched down, they should be able to get out. Eliza weighed the keys in her hand. From this point forward, they would need a lot of luck. *I hope the front door isn't noisy.*

Eliza glanced back over her shoulder and saw Millie staring at her hand, opening and closing her fist over and over again to create a tiny shower of rust-colored flakes. An alarm began to go off in her mind. *What am I doing? Millie might need some serious help. If I take her away, she may not ever get it!*

The more she thought, the harder it became to concentrate. The same chilling melody from her dreams twisted through her mind. *What was I worried about? Millie, Millie, something about Millie.* Whatever she had been worried about, it didn't matter; they had to get out. Everything would be okay once they got out. This wasn't a good place for them.

"Come on, we don't have much time left," Eliza whispered, taking a step toward her distracted friend.

"How do we get out?" Millie asked, her voice listless.

Eliza pulled the door back once more, edging her toe across the threshold. "We'll crouch down and run to the door. Then I'll stick in the key and we're out!" she explained, and her heart began to race. She crept forward as an unfamiliar song filled her mind.

Round the bend and under the tree
That's where we wait for thee
Come back to us and dance tonight
The ritual calls to please and delight

She had to get to the door.

The woman behind the desk didn't look up as they slid into the lobby and the door clicked shut behind them.

"Hey, what are you up to?" a deep voice boomed across the lobby.

Eliza froze, sucking in her breath.

Pithy laughter erupted, accompanied by the sharp clatter of bouncing keys. One of the younger guards was flirting with the receptionist. Her face was blocked by his muscular frame, but her high-pitched laughter continued to echo off the tile floor.

Not risking even a whisper, Eliza clutched Millie's hand a little tighter and tugged, signaling to begin walking once again.

Moments later, the pair reached the sealed set of double doors. Gripping the key in her sweaty palm, Eliza raised it to the lock and paused. The guard had led the receptionist around the corner.

Satisfied, she turned back to the task at hand. Sliding the gold key into the similar shade lock, Eliza slipped her bottom lip in-between her teeth as she turned it to the right, hearing a heavy clink as the lock gave way.

Beside her, Millie inhaled sharply but no siren exploded or cages came falling down around them.

Contrary to what she thought would happen, the door didn't open automatically. Instead, Eliza leaned to the right and applied a small amount of pressure, causing the door to slide open. Holding it, she gestured for Millie to race through.

Grunting, Eliza held the heavy door in place with one hand while trying to free the key with the other. Hopefully, when she pulled the key out, the door wouldn't slam shut.

"Eliza...where are you?" Millie hissed.

"I'm coming," Eliza replied, a large smile spreading across her face as she freed the key. Luckily the door remained open, beckoning her to step through. With one last glance at the distracted pair behind her, Eliza's smiled turned up at the corners maniacally. *We did it! We're out!*

Suddenly a shockingly loud alarm blared and red lights flashed. Eliza was halfway through the door when it groaned and slid away from her, causing her to lose her balance and fall forward.

"Eliza!" Millie cried.

With a startled gasp, Eliza rolled with the momentum and landed on her side a few feet away. "Whoa!"

Inside, both the guard and the receptionist were racing around, clutching their walkie-talkies. Eliza scrambled to her feet, her white tennis shoes making a satisfying slap against the cement sidewalk. After weeks of sterile tile, the scratchy texture made her heart sing.

The girls ran around the corner, out of sight from the clear doors. Eliza wasn't sure why the fire alarm went off but she knew what was going to happen next. Several minutes later a chorus of shouting voices and shrill cries filled the afternoon as a flood of patients and staff poured out the front doors.

Taking advantage of the chaos, Eliza nudged Millie and together they joined the melee, blending in with all the other patients in white shirts in seconds. Keeping a tight hold on Millie, Eliza directed them across the sidewalk toward the visitor's lot.

A few steps later they had reached the lot and found the dark green station wagon Sister Emily drove. Eliza guided Millie toward the back of the car recalling the hatchback window had been broken the last time she rode in it. Likely the Matron hadn't paid to fix it yet.

Eliza pressed her fingers experimentally against the dusty glass, and smiled when it bounced under her touch. She edged her fingers under and lifted the window, piercing the air with a horrendous screech as the rusted hinges protested.

In unison, both girls sucked in their breath, expecting to hear shouts. But the incessant ringing of the alarm still bellowed inside the hospital, covering them.

"Here, get inside. She might be here any minute," Eliza hissed. She helped Millie onto the bumper and into the trunk area, then followed, letting the window slam shut behind her as she landed on the stained carpet floor. She motioned for Millie to lay flat on her back. They did not need a patient, nurse or guard spotting them through the window.

Eliza exhaled loudly and laughed. "Mills! We made it! We're going to get away from this place!" She laughed again, then turned to look at her friend. "Millie! Aren't you happy?"

Millie stared at the stained ceiling of the car, her expression blank. Her lips moved silently.

"What did you say?" Eliza asked, feeling her happy glow diminishing by her friend's lack of enthusiasm.

"Why did that alarm go off?" Millie said, louder this time.

"Because...ah I don't know actually," Eliza admitted. She hadn't had time to think about that. Whatever the reason, it had proven helpful. She should have planned to pull the fire alarm in the first place.

"Do you think they found him?" Millie asked, her voice flat.

Eliza bit her lower lip as the picture of Jason's body, slumped on the tile in a pool of his own blood, filled her mind. They should have moved him, pulled his body out of plain sight. Alarms began to blare in her mind. They would discover she and Millie were missing, and they would know.

"Millie, we need to get out of here, out of the car now! They know we're gone, they know what we did!" Eliza half-screamed, struggling to rise to her knees in the small space.

"Eliza, stop—"

Eliza continued to move about the wagon, shaking it with her agitated movements.

"Eliza, please, stop," Millie said again, this time louder. *"Eliza!"*

Eliza stopped, her arms extended toward the glass. Millie hadn't raised her voice above a whisper since they had arrived at Belle Rose, and she couldn't recall her friend ever yelling at her before.

"Wh—"

"Shh!" Millie hissed. "Someone's coming!"

Eliza looked toward the main entrance. Sister Emily was making her way across the parking lot, her arms wrapped around her torso as though trying to make herself as small as possible as she wove through the crowd.

"Get down, hurry," Eliza commanded, pushing Millie. She didn't have time to wonder how Millie had known. Her heart was hammering and she could hear the blood rushing in her ears. There was no time to escape the car now, and no blankets or bags to help conceal them. They were stuck.

The front door opened loudly, screeching like the window had.

"Can't believe this...first I lose my keys, then the fire alarm goes off. She's going to kill me," Sister Emily groaned to herself as she started up the engine.

With a spurt and a stutter the car coughed to life and Sister Emily backed out of the parking space and then hit the gas, mumbling the entire time.

In the back, Eliza allowed herself to relax, letting the tension she held within her limbs seep into the dirty carpet. She heard the piercing cry of firetrucks headed toward the hospital as they sped away. They hadn't found Jason's body. The alarm may have even been a drill.

She moved to grin at Millie, but her friend had turned her head away. It didn't matter. They were free. She was going to get her friend back. And once they reached the swamps, everything would be okay.

A BOOMING CLAP of thunder startled Eliza awake. Blinking against the gray light, she tried to remember when she had fallen asleep, but her thoughts were murky. They were still moving, so they must not have arrived at St. Agatha's.

"Millie," Eliza whispered, her voice barely audible. Gently she touched her friend's shoulder but Millie didn't react. She must have fallen asleep as well.

"And we're back," Sister Emily's deflated voice suddenly rang out.

The station wagon bumped and swayed as Sister Emily turned off the main road and started down the unkempt dirt path that led to the orphanage.

Chancing a quick peek, Eliza rolled onto her side and propped herself up on her elbow to look out the window. Up ahead, St. Agatha's loomed like a dark flower blossoming against the pale sky, the towering spires climbing and twisting like giant vines. The darkening clouds billowed and grumbled in the distance; a storm would be on top of them soon.

Slowing to a crawl, the car bumped along the uneven gravel until it finally jerked to a stop several yards away from the large staircase leading to the front doors. Collecting her purse, Sister Emily took a steadying breath and then pushed open the door, closing it gently behind her. Eliza listened for her footsteps and the slam of the heavy wooden front door before sitting up.

"Millie, come on! We're here! Let's get out before Sister Mary comes out," Eliza hissed. She peeked out of the dirty window for any sign of movement, then glanced back at her friend and yelped in surprise. Millie was sitting up, her spine ramrod straight, her silver eyes blazing, and her lips moving rapidly.

"Millie, are you okay?" Eliza whispered.

Raspy words that Eliza couldn't understand tumbled from Millie's mouth, the sound sparking something deep within Eliza's mind.

Memories, dozens of forgotten memories suddenly assaulted Eliza, flickering and playing before her eyes like a movie.

There was a little dark haired boy, a girl with white blonde hair, and another girl with light brown skin. All of them had been innocent, happy until they met Eliza. Things had changed.

Violence stole their innocence; their eyes dulled and the color faded, leaving nothing but a silver void behind. And then they were gone.

Eliza's heart began to pound rapidly, trying to beat out of her body. She couldn't have, couldn't have corrupted those kids. But the memories disagreed.

Did you think you could change? Did you think you could forget?

Eliza closed her eyes and tried to block the velvety voice weaving through her mind.

You can never get away from us. We found you, saved you and now it's time for you to save us

"Come on, Mills! I won't let this happen again!" Eliza cried, grabbing her friend's wrist and pushing open the back window. She scrambled out, scraping her arms and legs on sharp edges. Millie didn't move until Eliza grabbed her by her underarms and pulled.

Their feet on the ground, they ran around the side of the car, hiding from any eyes that might look out the windows. The storm had arrived, announcing itself with a flash of lightening followed by a percussion of thunder. Eliza flinched. Millie remained upright, seemingly both blind and deaf to the world around her.

Surveying the landscape around her, Eliza was greeted by only tall trees and heavy moss blankets. St. Agatha's was located in the swamps for a reason; it was a difficult place to run away from.

Eliza knew the fairies would find them, stop them if they ran into the swamps. It was almost a mile walk to the road. They could make it, but if Sister Mary still planned on leaving like Sister Emily had mentioned, she would spot them instantly.

They didn't seem to have much of a choice. Eliza would have to protect Millie this time, save her from the same fate. She slipped her hand into Millie's and pulled her across the driveway toward the trees. The wind was picking up, howling angrily as it swirled around them. It kicked the loose dirt up, stinging their eyes. Holding one arm out as a shield, Eliza ran toward the haven the trees offered, yanking Millie after her.

A minute later the girls ducked underneath the swaying trees, running several feet further until Eliza felt they were safely out of sight. She let go of Millie's hand and watched it fall limply to her friend's side.

More unintelligible words spilled from Millie's lips, her volume and intensity increasing with the wind. The language she spoke was gibberish; exotic, yet completely familiar. The harsh syllables made Eliza cringe.

Millie's eyes began to roll around in their sockets until she was staring up at the twisting branches above them. Goose bumps prickled Eliza's skin, not from the thunder rolling overhead, but the quiet voices she could now hear whispering. No matter how she tried to focus, the poisonous words continued to trickle in, filling her mind.

Bring her to us. You know the place. Bring her to us

Tears poured from the corners of Eliza's eyes, hot on her cheeks. She wouldn't give in, would not let them take Millie. This time she would make it, she would be able to resist.

"Millie, we need to get to the road before they can...Millie!" Eliza screamed into the wind, but her friend was gone. Spinning in a tight circle, Eliza scanned the trees for any sign of her. Nothing but trembling branches greeted her search. "*Millie!*"

A flash of white fluttered in her peripheral vision. "Millie, wait!" Eliza called, stumbling over raised roots in that direction. "Millie!"

Millie didn't stop and disappeared around a thick trunk, headed deep into the swamp.

"No!"

She had to save her, had to get her back before Millie found the fairies. Eliza took off at a sprint, ducking and swatting low hanging branches and curtains of moss out of her way.

Memory after memory bubbled before her as she ran. The little boy smiling as she held his hand, leading him into the woods behind their foster parents' house. The little black-haired girl staring up in wonder as the fairies descended. The blonde child crying as the fairies closed in, blocking her from Eliza's view. Although she hadn't seen, Eliza knew what fate the children had met, what fate Eliza had led them to.

Millie was going to die.

CHAPTER

12

B RING HER TO us
Bring her to the realm
You know how

Silken words surrounded Eliza, the soft voice tempting and hypnotic. Her feet involuntarily shuffled forward.

"No! I won't let you take her!" Eliza sobbed, grabbing onto a nearby branch to stop herself.

You can't stop us
We will find her
She's looking for us
You'll come too, you always do, you always watch

"Millie!" Eliza cried, frantically scanning the darkening, thick wood for her friend. She knew it was no use. The fairies would find her, they always did.

The memories flooded out of her subconscious, playing like a movie in her head. It was the same every time. Find a hopeful child, gain their trust, and bury them deep.

Crimson images splattered the trees around her. They attacked until there was nothing left, nothing but horrific memories.

Eliza released the branch, regaining herself for a moment, and sprinted forward, choosing a direction at random. She had to fight them, had to find Millie and save her before it was too late.

The fairies closed in as she ran, and Eliza saw her past play out like a movie around her. Displayed between mossy bald cypress trees was herself at five years old, discovering the fairies for the first time.

"Go pee, Eliza, hurry now," her mother said with a patient smile, waving her away.

"But I don't want anyone to see me," Eliza said as she hopped up and down.

"Okay, why don't you go behind that tree?" her mother offered, pointing to a large tree set farther back from the road.

"Okay," Eliza said hesitantly. She pushed open the door. "Can you turn up the radio?" It was scary outside.

"Sure sweetie, go on," her mom said, turning the volume of the happy song way up.

Eliza nodded and jumped out, her sneakers sinking into the squishy ground when she landed. She picked her way across the field to the tree, hurried behind it and pulled down her pants. She felt so much better.

Squealing tires screamed and her happy song was cut off. Eliza looked up in a panic and yanked her pants back up. "Mama?" she called out.

Eliza came around the tree and saw the red car dashing away, leaving her on the side of the abandoned road. "Mama," she cried, the tears already running down her cheeks. "Mama! Come back!" She took a few steps and slipped on the wet ground, falling. The dampness quickly seeped into her pants. "Mama, come back! Don't leave me!"

She struggled to stand again, but the taillights had disappeared. "Mama!" Eliza screamed, tears blinding her as she ran. She didn't see the dip in the ground and went sprawling into the dirt, her ankle twisting.

"Mama, help me! Come back," Eliza cried into the darkening sky, but no one answered. Her tiny chest heaved up and down as her breathing raged out of control. Why wasn't her mama turning around?

Eliza sat on the wet ground for hours, waiting for the red car to come back, for her mother to realize that she had forgotten her. But she never came.

She didn't know how long she lay there in the mud and leaves, but eventually she had cried all her tears and her mind was made up. If Mama wasn't coming back, then she would have to find her.

Eliza limped along the side of the road for some time, the trees surrounding the lone stretch growing denser. At last she saw a bright light sparkle in the shrubbery and hope blossomed. Her mama had come back with a flashlight.

"Mom! Mom I'm over here!" she bellowed, charging into the woods.

The light grew brighter the further Eliza walked. It looked like it was coming from behind a tall tree. Eliza swatted through the branches until she reached it. She clung to the trunk, climbed around the tree and stepped into the light. "Mama!" she cried.

No one was there. The light she had seen was moonlight, reflecting off a small bog rippling at the base of the tree. It looked like a giant, silver mirror.

The truth hit Eliza like a boxing glove to the gut. "No," she whispered as fresh tears clouded her vision. Her mom wasn't there, she wasn't looking for her. She had left her on purpose.

Blinded by tears and grief, Eliza stumbled, slipping on the wet grass. She reached out for something to stall her fall, her tiny fingers finding nothing substantial. She screamed as her body hit the stagnant water with a great splash, and her cry was cut off as she went under.

Fear seized her gut and froze her limbs. She couldn't swim. An alligator could be hiding below.

Eliza kicked and thrashed at the water, but it was useless. Her limbs began to tire and her chin kept dipping below the surface, the algae slipping into her mouth and clogging her nose. If she could reach the bank, she could pull herself out. But her arms felt like lead and she couldn't keep her head above the surface any longer.

Plunging to the silt covered floor, a stream of bubbles escaped Eliza's lips as the last of her air whooshed out of her lungs. Her body began to jerk, instinctually fighting for air. Black spots fizzled before her eyes as her body depleted the rest of the oxygen, and her brain started to shut down.

The water held her eyelids open. As she drowned, Eliza was vaguely aware of a halo of silver light approaching. Had she found heaven?

The small black dots grew larger as her body surrendered, her lungs still burning for air. She felt her shoes hit the bottom of the bog. It would be over soon.

Just as the darkness took over the last of her vision, Eliza noticed several more silver bursts straining toward her. If she could make it to the light, she would be safe.

The blackness covered her eyes then and the burning stopped as her body lay dead at the bottom of the swamp.

Eliza pushed her legs to go faster as the memories continued to flit past her. At five years old, she had thought that was it, her end, the end of her short life.

Moments after her heart gave its final beat, she awoke on the edge of the bank, coughing and sputtering the putrid water from her lungs.

Her head fell to the side, water still dribbling out of her mouth as she gulped in the glorious, moist air around her. She was alive; somehow she had gotten out, escaped the blackness.

Pressing her palms into the soft mud at her sides, Eliza pushed her body up and sat hunched over, rubbing her small hand along the base of her throat as she remembered the burning sensation while she struggled to breathe.

She had died, she was sure of it. How did she get out? Had her mother found her after all? "Mama?" Eliza called hopefully, but only silence greeted her. She looked around, but the woods remained quiet save for the early rustlings of the forest as the squirrels curled up in their nests and the nocturnal creatures awakened.

Then she heard a gentle rustling and turned to look over her shoulder. Floating delicately around her were tiny creatures, all painted with sparkling silver skin and ebony shadows. She felt a tickle of fear as they smiled down at her, waving their tiny fingers.

"Hello, little one. It is all right, there is no need to be frightened," the beautiful creatures sang. "We're fairies. Would you like to stay with us?"

Eliza nodded, reaching out her small hand to touch a fairy's wings. They looked like a spider web, trailing far below the rest of her body as she fluttered out of Eliza's reach.

"Yes please," Eliza whispered.

"That's a good girl," the fairy smiled, her tiny tongue running along her lower lip. "We'll protect you."

"Thank you," Eliza said, rising to her feet as she accepted a brightly colored piece of fruit. She brought the fruit to her lips and took a bite. It was the most delicious thing she had ever tasted.

"Welcome to the realm," the fairy said, running her thin fingers through Eliza's matted hair.

The memory faded once more back to the present, but the same voice followed her.

We saved you little one, protected you from the final shadow
We watched over you and kept you safe
All we asked was your help in return

Eliza shook her head, trying to shake the voice from her thoughts.

We crave life and energy to survive
Blood is the only matter that can sustain us
But we can't find it on our own
We asked for a simple favor
One child every two years and we shall share our every lasting life with you
We shall be your family
But still you resist

Eliza's foot caught and she tripped, falling against a tree. More images clouded her mind. "Just leave me alone!" Eliza screamed, pressing the heel of her hand to her temple. Through the haze of voices filling her thoughts, she saw a flash of color. Millie.

"Millie, wait! They'll catch you!" Eliza screamed, scrambling to her feet and resuming her sprint. Another memory blinded her as she ran.

"Eliza, where are we going?" little James whined as Eliza clasped his tiny hand in hers.

"It's not much farther," Eliza promised, swinging their joined arms. "We're pirates remember? We can't go back without our buried treasure."

She continued to walk, leading him farther from the small yard of her new foster home. Jim and Nicole seemed nice enough. Hopefully she could stay here.

"Look, right there, James!" Eliza pointed to a large curled tree. Its trunk had been hollowed out and a dark black hole beckoned them forward. They crept closer and numerous silver lights glistened within, shining like stars in the night sky.

James stopped walking, shaking his head. "No, Eliza. We need to go back. Jim said it was dinnertime soon," he pleaded in his small voice.

"But it's an adventure! Come on James, just a little farther. They're waiting for you," Eliza said excitedly, gripping his hand tighter.

"But I don't like them," James sniffled, pointing to the silver lights. "They're bad."

"Don't be silly," Eliza told him, bending down to grab a nearby stick. She let go of James' hand and smiled. "They're friends of mine."

She broke the stick in half, creating two sharp points. Eliza let one half drop to the ground and held the other one firmly.

"Now, to get the treasure you need to make a sacrifice, a blood sacrifice," Eliza explained, taking James' hand once again. "This will hurt."

James' lip trembled as he tried to pull away, but Eliza held fast. With a quick stab, she sliced James' palm with the sharp stick, drawing bright red blood.

"Ow!" James cried, yanking his hand away and holding it to his chest. "I'm telling Jim!" The little boy turned to run, but Eliza blocked his path and pushed him down. He landed on his back, stunned.

The fairies arrived. Eliza stepped back, allowing the silver creatures to gather and enclose James in a tight silver bubble. All she could see were his little sneakers.

James had worn sneakers that lit up with every step. They had never lit up again.

"Well done, child," the fairies whispered.

Eliza nodded, smiling as she watched the fairies lick their spidery wings clean. All that remained of James were his sneakers. Eliza tossed them into the nearest bog, watching with disinterest as they sank below the surface. "No one will ever find you," she sang, then turned and skipped back to the house. Dinner would be served soon.

The fairies had buried that memory deep.

"Eliza, we're losing our patience," Jim growled. "Where is James?"

"Who's James?" Eliza asked, wiping her face and confused by the presence of tears.

"Stop this!" Nicole yelled, grabbing onto Eliza's shoulders and shaking her. "Where is he? My son went into the woods with you!"

Eliza didn't understand. She was their only child. "I don't know what you're saying! I don't know what's going on!"

Jim separated Nicole from Eliza and locked Eliza away in a small bedroom. They kept her in there all night, even when the cars with the sirens and lights came. Eliza watched from the window as the police combed the yard and woods. She wondered what they were looking for.

Eliza picked up her pace. She would save Millie. She wouldn't let it happen again. She would not forget Millie like she had forgotten Julia and Harmony. They had been older, and required more convincing.

More hidden memories ignited one after another, playing back the past in vivid color. She remembered it now, remembered chasing after them, leading them to the realm. The fairies had only showed magic and beauty. It was too easy to convince her friends that the realm was a better place than their foster home. They fell for it every time.

Once they visited the realm, the fairies ignited the silver powder and invaded the intended child's mind, driving them mad with whisperings and impossible tomorrows until they forgot the real world. Their eyes had turned to silver and Eliza led them back to the swamp.

And now, it was Millie's turn.

With that thought, a switch flipped inside Eliza.

The heavy guilt that had been sitting atop her shoulders vanished as her memories returned full circle.

She loved the fairies, was a part of the realm herself. What was Millie? *An abandoned girl at St. Agatha's.* The fairies had saved her life; it was time to repay them.

A slow smile spread across Eliza's lips as her eyes searched the trees. She was no longer trying to save Millie. She had become a hunter.

Welcome back, pet

Make us proud

The voices purred, functioning like a command. Eliza moved forward, her eyes sweeping the landscape before her. She would find Millie. She would find her and bring her to the circle where the fairies could complete the ritual.

M ILLIE?" ELIZA CALLED, her voice sweet. "Come out come out wherever you are!" She glided over the grass, unaffected as the skies opened, drenching her hair and clothes. Her eyelashes fought to remain open under the weight.

Prompted forward by the melodious songs the fairies sang, Eliza wandered on until she saw, a spot of bright white crouched between the thick roots of a bald cypress tree.

Eliza's wet sneakers squished on the ground and her toes curled as she hurried forward, her heart beating calmly against her ribcage. Placing her palm on the rough bark, Eliza bent down and smiled widely.

Millie hunched underneath the raised trunk, her silver eyes shut tightly and her teeth gnashed together. Her clothes weren't wet. She had been hiding under there for a while.

"What are you doing under there, Mills?" Eliza asked, her smile growing wider. "Are you okay?"

Raising her head off the muddy grass and relaxing out of the fetal position, Millie looked around, blindly trying to locate her friend. There was fear in her expression. "Eliza?" she whispered.

"Come on, let's get you out of there," Eliza said lightly, reaching down for Millie's hand. "You scared me. I thought I wasn't going to be able to find you."

Millie let Eliza pull her out of her hiding place. Eliza noticed goose bumps prickling her skin. "Oh, Millie," she teased, cocking her head. "You left me, after everything I did to get you out of that place!"

The rain hammered the trees and the ground around them, soaking Millie.

Eliza waited for her to say something, but she didn't. It didn't matter. It was time to go.

"Come with me," Eliza told her, reaching out to take Millie by the hand once more. Millie flinched away and took a step back. Eliza narrowed her eyes and left her arm suspended in the air, her sleeve quickly becoming saturated with water. "What are you doing?"

"Something is wrong, Liza," Millie whispered.

"Wrong?" Eliza laughed. "What could be wrong?" She took another step toward Millie as her friend backed away.

"What did you do to me?" Millie shouted, her fingers rubbing her temple. "What did you tell me to do? How did their voices get back inside my head?" She bent forward, digging her fingernails into her scalp, and let out a guttural cry.

Eliza smiled and closed the distance between them. She reached a hand out to rub Millie's back but paused and hovered an inch above her. "I didn't tell you to do anything," she said quietly.

"Yes you did, someone did. Someone told me to pick up the toilet cover, showed me—in my head...how to hit him...told me I had to do it...made me—!" Millie shouted, silver tears running down her face. "What are you?"

Eliza let her hand fall to Millie's back but the other girl twisted away from her touch. Eliza sighed and crossed her arms. "I didn't do anything, Mills. I took away your pills and gave you the opportunity to listen, to find them. But you could have resisted. You didn't want to. You need them, just as much as I do." She smiled.

"But I can't...I can't remember...silver dancers...you-you brought me to them and showed me...and tried, you t-tried to s-stop them before," Millie stuttered.

"But that was before," Eliza said, running her hand along the wet bark of a nearby tree. The heavy rain was beginning to lighten up, the heavy Louisiana heat returning.

"Before what? Eliza, what is going on? What are you doing?" Millie cried, the silver powder in her eyes shimmering with full force now that the fairies were so near. All Eliza had to do was enter the realm and the ritual would begin.

Eliza shrugged. "Does it matter? I showed you what you needed to see, did what I needed to do. Yes, I admit I had a momentary lapse in my beliefs but they showed me where I belong and what is truly important in this life."

Millie began to sob, her shoulders heaving up and down. "Are you—g-going to kill me?"

"No, Mills," Eliza sighed softly. "But they are."

Spinning in a tight circle, she jerked her arm across a large bush covered in thorns. She felt the trickle of blood before she saw it. Several shallow gashes decorated her skin.

Eliza held her arm out and suddenly dozens of silver fairies sparkled out of thin air, all converging on her arm, their silver tongues flashing as they lapped up the spilling blood. The noise of their tongues created a sickening melody.

Millie turned to run and collided with a low hanging branch. She stumbled back into Eliza, causing the fairies to alight into the air.

Eliza smiled and reached into the thorn bush, snapping off a short section of one of the curling stems.

Wrapping her left arm around Millie's throat, Eliza crushed her friend into her and brought her other hand clutching the thorns up. Millie fought wildly, but Eliza held tight, angling the thorns. She gritted her teeth and sent the branch up and across, leaving three large cuts along Millie's nose and cheek.

Millie screamed, falling to her knees and clutching her cheek. "Eliza, what are you doing?" Blood seeped out from between her fingers, running down her arm. "I thought you wanted to be free, to run away and find a family," she sobbed.

Eliza smiled wolfishly and bent down so that she was eye-level with her friend. "I already have a family," she giggled.

Millie stumbled away from Eliza, her tears running red down her face.

"Where are you going, Mills?" Eliza called out cheerfully, following a few steps behind.

"Don't call me that!" Millie yelled.

Eliza scoffed and feigned a hurt look. "Aw Mills, it's all right. The pain will stop in a few minutes. We just have to wait for the rain to stop, then they'll come, just like you wanted. Remember?"

Millie shook her head and fell against a nearby tree, her small arms trying to wrap around the slick trunk. "I don't remember anything, my head...it hurts," she said, closing her eyes. "I think...I think I did something bad."

"I think that can happen," Eliza said with a frown. "The body can only withstand the venom for so long."

"What are you talking about?" Millie asked.

"Your eyes. Haven't you noticed?" Eliza asked mockingly. "You did kill Jason back at the asylum. Don't you remember how *red* his blood was?"

Millie sucked in her breath as sobs began to rack her body. Eliza smiled. Now that they were in the realm, there was no need for any more magic.

The venom had caused Millie's eyes to change and taken away her sense of consciousness. The pills the nurses had tried to give her every night attempted to bring her back, and Eliza had fixed that.

Quietly she snuck up on the other side of the tree and brushed her fingers along Millie's skin.

Millie jerked away at the unexpected touch, slipping down the tree trunk. She dug her heels into the grass, stopping her slide just before her sneakers touched the rippling water of a bog.

"Oh Millie," Eliza sighed, lowering to a crouch. "Did you think it would just go away, that your sight would magically come back?" She laughed, wiggling her fingers. "You made us a promise. Now it's time to collect."

Millie turned her head away from an invisible attacker.

Eliza chuckled as she watched one of the fairies appear just above Millie's shoulder. Her long silver tongue whipped up and ran up Millie's bleeding cheek.

Others appeared as payment was accepted. Their spidery wings flapped lazily as they descended from the air, their shadowy dresses charcoal smudges against the gray sky. Eliza tilted her head as they whispered to her. It wouldn't be long now.

"Eliza, please," Millie whispered, tears still running down her face. "You're my friend."

Eliza turned back and looked down to where Millie sat, her small fingers digging into the wet hillside to keep from slipping into the swamp below.

Her smile widened. "But they're my family," she replied coldly.

Millie's mouth opened but no sound came out. "Are they going to kill me now?" she cried, her lips trembling.

Eliza's cold laugh echoed throughout the swamp, reverberating off the dark trees. "Yes," she growled and lunged forward, grabbing Millie by the shoulder and wrenching her back up the small embankment.

"Eliza, no!" Millie screamed, her cry piercing the calm woods around her.

Several crows cawed and alighted into the air, startled by the sound. The fairies flew closer, the black shadows smeared across their bodies billowing sensually in the warm breeze. A thin coating of mist cloaked their webby wings, glistening, disguising the true horror beneath.

With a heavy grunt, Eliza wrapped her other hand around Millie's long brown and silver- streaked hair.

"No! Stop it, please, Liza, stop!" Millie sobbed, her hands fluttering uselessly against Eliza's hold.

Eliza heaved Millie back up the small slope and dropped her, knocking the wind out of the smaller girl. Millie stopped crying as she tried to catch her breath. She scrambled to her hands and knees, attempting to crawl away.

"Oh no you don't," Eliza giggled, wrenching her friend back by her hair once more. Millie landed hard on her back and didn't move. "We have things to do. The realm can't wait for you any longer."

Grabbing Millie by the muddy ankles, Eliza began to pull her further into the swamp as the whispering of the fairies increased in intensity. They were getting restless.

She pulled Millie's body into a clearing between the trees and bogs and let her friend drop with a wet thud. Millie sat up weakly, tears streaming down her face. Blood and mud coated her as she fumbled blindly for a means to escape. Her fingers closed on something and she pulled it from the muck.

Bending down, Eliza retrieved it and wiped the thick mud away.

The memory of a little doll with brown hair danced across Eliza's vision. Millie had carried the doll into the swamp with her the first time they entered the realm. The day the fairies had chosen her.

With a short laugh, Eliza tossed the broken doll arm back into the mud where it landed with a soft squish. "That doll. Remember you thought the doll looked like you, Mills?" Eliza chuckled. "Soon you'll be twins."

Millie's breathing hitched and she hugged her knees to her chest, rocking back and forth. A burst of pity erupted inside Eliza as she stared at the frightened girl. For a moment she softened, remembering their dreams of running away.

The gentle touch of a fairy's wings shifted her attention back to the present, back to the mud.

The fairy stared at her, her silver smile confident, trusting. Eliza had a job to do; her family couldn't wait any longer.

The other fairies followed languidly behind the girls, their songs growing louder with anticipation. Eliza smiled at the one closest to her and nodded, ready to begin the ritual.

The ground was a little firmer where Eliza stood. It would make a good spot to watch from.

Brushing her wet hair out of her face, Eliza sighed and bent down behind Millie, threading her arms under hers and hoisting the girl back onto her feet.

"Come on, Mills. Time to get moving," Eliza groaned under her weight.

"Liza, please. Don't do this. Just let me go. I promise I won't tell, I won't tell anyone. Just let me go," Millie cried, her limbs refusing to cooperate as Eliza tried to pick her off the ground.

Eliza huffed and groaned as she used all of her strength to set Millie on her feet. Her friend sagged forward, forcing Eliza to stumble as she caught her. "Don't make this harder than it has to be, Mills," Eliza hissed through gritted teeth. "It'll all be over soon."

Millie's tears started again as she held tightly onto Eliza's hand. "Please," she begged again.

Eliza grimaced and shook Millie's hand away. "You should be grateful," she said soothingly. "You're going to see your family soon. Don't you want that?"

Millie continued to cry.

"You'll see," Eliza said with a reassuring smile.

Humming with the fairies, Eliza maneuvered Millie into a standing position just under a large branch. A curtain of moss blew lazily above them, the soft silver tendrils reaching out to brush the tops of their heads.

"Okay, so now the hard part's over. You just need to stand here and they'll do the rest," Eliza instructed brightly, as if she were teaching Millie how to rollerblade.

Millie raised her head and stared at Eliza, her silver eyes shining like the fairies around them. She didn't say anything, didn't cry any longer. She waited.

Eliza smiled, her lips pulling up at the corner of her mouth just slightly. She wiggled her fingers goodbye to her friend. It would all be over soon and she could forget again, forget everything.

A tiny flame of guilt sparked to life once more as she backed away from Millie.

One, two, three steps away, another friend gone, another friend left alone.

Four, five, six, she looked so small standing by herself.

Seven, eight, nine, the storm clouds were gathering again as the fairies' songs built. Any second and it would be over.

Ten...

The fairies descended, a black and silver mass almost obscuring Millie completely. Eliza's throat constricted and she swallowed roughly. Maybe this time she wouldn't look. She could honor Millie that way. But as the song reached its climax and the silver smiles fell away to reveal the fairies' needle-sharp teeth, Eliza raised her eyes to the scene before her once more. She had to look, she always looked.

Goose bumps rose along Eliza's arms. "Bye, Mills," Eliza whispered, running her tongue over her bottom lip.

The sound of gnashing teeth replaced the chilling lullaby and Eliza felt her spine shiver in anticipation. As gruesome as it was, she was always a little excited. Her breathing picked up as the first fairy laid her lips on Millie's exposed collarbone. Just a few more seconds and the colors would change from silver to red.

Another fairy leaned in to also taste Millie's skin, but there was a sudden jerk within the circle as Millie rolled to the side, catching the fairies off guard.

"Millie, no!" Eliza yelled as Millie broke free and began sprinting through the trees. She took several steps forward, a small part of her willing Millie to get away. But she knew her fairies. No one ever got away.

The fairies attacked, teeth and nails bared, their sweet song transformed to raspy growls. This time there was no tenderness.

Thousands of teeth ripped into Millie's flesh, crazed and hurried like a pack of wolves feasting. Eliza was unable to look away as her friend was devoured piece by piece. Her scream was piercing, desperate as it echoed throughout the swamp.

Screaming never helped.

Within seconds the sparkling silver painting disintegrated, its perfection marred by a splattering of crimson. The ritual only took a few seconds. The air was still, the swamp silent now that Millie's screams no longer ran out.

Eliza meandered forward, drawn to the pooling blood seeping into the mud, running into the dark water. There was nothing left of her friend; even her tennis shoes had been torn to shreds.

The murky landscape surrounding Eliza suddenly burned bright as the realm absorbed Millie's energy, transforming once more to shining silver. She could feel the tips of her fingers tingling with energy as the shadows lengthened and the fairies licked their skin clean.

A soft rain picked up again, hitting the leaves with a gentle pitter-patter. Chills ran up Eliza's spine and she wrapped her arms around herself as she walked toward the last place Millie had been alive.

The dark red blood was already disappearing, the cold rain diluting it to a cloudy pink. Now that it was over, now that Eliza couldn't help even if she wanted to, she was overcome with crushing guilt.

This was her fourth payment. Four times she had gained someone's trust, told them it would be all right. Tears poured down her face as she sunk to her knees, her white pants becoming soaked with pink blood in seconds. She reached out and submerged her hands in the pool, trying to touch her friend, to connect one last time. It was too late; Millie was gone. The fairies had made certain of that.

Her fingers connected with something hard in the swirling pool. Millie's identification bracelet from Belle Rose.

Sitting back on her heels, Eliza let the broken bracelet slip from her fingers back into the blood, where it bobbed along the surface, Millie's name glaring accusingly back at her.

Come now, Eliza. This isn't any different than before

Eliza sniffled and wiped her running nose with the back of her hand. She felt the bloody water race down her neck and didn't try to mop it up. It wouldn't matter. The rain had begun to fall again.

"What have I done," Eliza whispered.

You saved us, saved the realm. You did the right thing

Eliza gripped her head in her hands and pressed as hard as she could, trying to force the images out.

It's always the same, Eliza. That's why we take the past away

The soft voices tried to placate her, soothe her sorrow, but they only made her feel worse. She never wanted to betray another friend, never wanted to forget the screams.

"No!" Eliza cried, leaping to her feet. The fairies backed away from her violent outburst, their delicate features confused.

Eliza took several steps away from the ruined shoes, suddenly desperate to get away and escape the realm. The fairies seemed to sense her anger and formed a tight ring around her.

"Get away from me!" Eliza screamed, throwing her arms out. Her wild punches sailed through several of them, their tiny bodies transforming to nothing more than spider webs.

Racing away from the circle, Eliza tried to shake the clinging webs off her fingers. She didn't know where she was heading or what she would do now that the memory of Millie would forever haunt her.

Come back to us
This won't help
You can never get away

A chorus of voices called sweetly after Eliza. She kept pumping her legs until the silver ferns and trees began to shimmer and fade back to dark browns and warm greens.

Eliza surged forward, knocking mossy curtains and branches away. Up ahead, she could see the tree line getting sparse and the dirt lane peeking out between the narrow trunks. She was almost out! Even the Matron seemed welcoming after the horror she had just participated in.

Ducking low, Eliza maneuvered one last thorn bush and stepped through the tree line. The moment her shoe hit the other side, a strange wave washed over her, freezing her movements.

You will never get away

The velvety voice wove through her mind one final time, taking all of Eliza's recent memories with it. Gone was the realm, gone were the fairies, gone was the blood, the car ride, the asylum, gone was Millie.

It was as if her mind had been wiped clean. One easy swipe and all of the terrifying memories evaporated, leaving Eliza alone, surrounded by nothing but blank space.

Her body resumed its fast pace and she stumbled, her feet getting mixed messages from her brain.

Why am I running? Where am I?

Wandering around, Eliza saw an ugly, dark green station wagon sitting in the long driveway. She walked closer and saw that a nun sat in the driver's seat, gaping at her.

"Hello? Can you tell me where I am?" Eliza called loudly through the rain.

The nun slowly opened the door and stepped out, her face pale, her expression horrified. "Eliza?" she whispered. "What have you done? What are you doing here?"

Eliza watched as the nun stumbled backward and sprinted up the large concrete steps. She was screaming, yelling at the top of her lungs. Eliza cocked her head to the side and followed her to the bottom of the front steps. The nun reacted strangely to a little girl.

The nun glanced over her shoulder and began to pound on the wooden doors, her words at last coming through to Eliza. "Matron! Matron, call the police! Call them now! Eliza is here!"

Eliza paused, her hand on the concrete banister, confused as she watched the scene before her unfold.

Spurred by the woman's shouts, several other nuns and young girls spilled out the front doors and onto the steps, all wearing the same look of confusion and fear. They gawked at her, their eyes wide as saucers. The younger children began to cry.

Eliza couldn't understand their reaction. She looked herself over. White shirt, white pants, and mud-caked sneakers. She peered closer. The white clothes were covered in rusty brown and bright red smears.

She held her damp shirt away from her body and her mind started to whirl. She was covered in blood! Head to toe, as if she had been rolling around in it. Eliza raked her mind for any memory of how she had gotten in this state. The last solid memory she had was of her caseworker saying Eliza had to leave the foster home. *Why won't the orphanage accept me?*

"What's going on?" Eliza asked, turning over her arms and twisting around to try and find the source of the blood. There was so much of it. Surely she must be cut somewhere, but she felt no pain.

She looked back at the stairs, straight into the terrified eyes of a tight-lipped woman.

"Hello," Eliza said, trying to smile, but the drying blood caked around her mouth made her skin feel tight.

"What have you done?" the woman asked, her voice shaking.

"What do you mean? Where am I?" Eliza asked, peering around the woman at the girls behind her. She had never seen any of them before.

"The police are on their way. Belle Rose, too," the woman said tightly, her gray eyes never blinking.

"Belle Rose? Who is she? Should I know her?" Eliza asked.

"Where did you leave her?" the woman asked, looking past Eliza toward the swamp.

"Leave who?" Eliza asked. She wanted to giggle. This woman must have her confused with someone else.

"Millie. Where did you leave her?" the woman demanded as her breathing hitched.

Eliza's eyes widened as she glanced around at the assembled girls surrounding her. "Is she one of them?" she wondered. The woman needed to relax. She was looking the wrong direction.

"Stop this! Just stop. That is enough!" the woman screamed, throwing her hands up. "Why did you kill her? Why couldn't you have just stayed away?"

"Kill her?" Eliza whispered, cocking her head to the side. "What are you talking about?"

Tears streamed down the woman's face. A pretty nun with large brown eyes placed a hand on the older woman's elbow. "Matron, please. Let me talk to her."

The Matron turned back to the girls behind her, attempting to usher them back up the stairs. The younger nun crouched in front of Eliza.

Eliza smiled as she looked down at the nun. She liked her. She could tell she was nice. "Hi, I'm Eliza," she said, extending her hand.

The nun bit her bottom lip as Eliza clasped her hand in her bloodied one. "Hello, Eliza. I'm Sister Emily. Do you think you can tell me what happened to Millie?" she asked.

"I don't know who she is," Eliza apologized. "I tried to tell the other lady that but she got mad."

Sister Emily nodded. "Yes, I saw. But do you think you could try really hard to remember? It's really important that we find her. She could be hurt."

Eliza put her hand to her head. She wanted to give the sweet nun an answer, but the only thing she could recall was stepping out of the trees and walking to the steps.

Closing her eyes, Eliza pictured herself in the woods. She liked playing in the woods. A blurry image of white and silver flashed across her mind, but before she could explore it further, it disintegrated and darkness took its place.

"I'm sorry, I don't know who Millie is," Eliza said again, releasing the breath she was holding. Frown lines appeared on Sister Emily's face.

The rain and all of the questions were suddenly too much for Eliza. "Do you think I can go inside and get some new clothes?"

Sister Emily hung her head. "I don't think so," she answered, and glanced over Eliza's shoulder.

Shrill cries and flashing lights suddenly shattered the quiet. Eliza turned and saw a dozen vehicles speeding down the muddy lane toward them. Red and blue lights of police cars and white and red sirens of ambulances roared down the driveway. Fear gripped her gut as men in white uniforms poured from the back of one of the ambulances.

"Eliza! Stay right there, all right, stay right there," a man shouted as police officers began spanning out across the grounds, accompanied by German shepherds. They were headed for the swamp.

"What's happening? Are they looking for someone?" Eliza asked, her smile faltering.

"Come on, Miss Eliza. Give us your hands real slow," a guard directed, his deep voice slow and steady.

Eliza looked up at him and then around, confused to see so many people in uniform surrounding her now.

A sharp *clink* brought Eliza's attention back to the man in front of her just as he was locking the heavy handcuffs in place. He tightened them as far as they would go, but they still hung from her small wrists.

Eliza frowned and looked for Sister Emily or one of the other girls, but they were gone. They were all gone.

Epilogue

"COME ON, MISS Eliza. Let's get you back to your room," a guard said, gently guiding her forward, his hand on the small of her back. His name tag read Leroy.

Eliza glanced around at the stark white hallways, each one an exact replica of the last. It wasn't a pleasant place. Leroy stopped before a shiny silver door and pressed a round button, illuminating it to a dull orange glow.

"We're not taking the stairs?" Eliza wondered out loud as they heard the elevator whirring to life.

Leroy glanced down at her but didn't say anything, returning his gaze upward to the brightly lit number 4 as the elevator began its descent.

As they waited for the doors to slide open, another guard accompanying an older girl with short black hair and green eyes joined them.

Eliza gave the new pair a bright smile.

The guard looked away to greet Leroy, but the girl stared back at Eliza, her eyes wide and her jaw slack.

"What are you doing back here?" she hissed. "I thought you got out?"

Eliza frowned. "What are you talking about?"

Both guards looked at them, suspicion in their eyes.

Jackie stepped away from Eliza, which seemed to placate them just as the elevator doors pinged open.

"In you go," Leroy instructed, giving Eliza a gentle push to the back of the dark box.

The distorted image of another dark space caused Eliza's heart to quicken, and she found herself scared. She stepped into the far corner and began humming. The other girl positioned herself next to Eliza and hissed, "The fire alarm didn't work? I thought it would help."

Eliza frowned again. "What are you talking about? Who are you?"

"Jackie, enough," the other guard said, stepping between them. "Don't talk to her."

"But how is she back here? What happened to her? She knows me," Jackie said angrily, throwing up her hands.

"It doesn't concern you," her guard said sternly.

"Tell me, tell me why she doesn't remember me," Jackie insisted. Her guard moved, blocking Eliza's view. Leroy came to stand in front of Eliza, doubling the screen.

"Why is she yelling?" Eliza asked, peering around Leroy's big frame.

"Quiet," Leroy said, shifting to block her view.

"What's going on? Where's the other one, the one with the silver eyes? Why isn't she with you?" Jackie cried, her voice becoming frantic.

"That's enough, Jackie," the guard said, as the doors opened onto the third floor. Eliza watched through the gap between Leroy's elbow and body as the guard wrestled Jackie into the hallway.

"Melanie or Molly, where is she? Is she still out?" Jackie called, kicking and twisting her body to try and break the guard's hold.

"Millie?" Eliza called back, standing on her tiptoes to keep the girl in view.

"Yes! She got out with you, right? So I did help! But why did you come back?" Jackie questioned, the desperation on her face clear as the guard tried to drag her away.

Leroy grabbed onto Eliza's shoulder, steering her out of the elevator and in the opposite direction. Jackie still struggled against her guard and Eliza felt bad. Jackie was worried about Millie, like everyone else seemed to be.

"They think I killed her," she called. "But I don't remember."

Jackie stopped fighting. "But she was your friend," she whispered.

Eliza's giddiness fled and her face turned cold. She couldn't remember much about that day, but she was certain of one thing. "I don't have any friends," Eliza told her, and gladly allowed Leroy to hurry her away.

"She is dangerous, Jackie," the guard said.

A sense of calm overcame Eliza as she and Leroy turned down another hallway, stopping beside the sixth white door on the right.

"In you go, Miss Eliza. The doctor will be in to talk to you soon," Leroy said gently, unlocking the heavy door with the key attached to his belt.

Eliza smiled up at him, happy again, and crossed the threshold into the white room. She spun in a circle before settling on the edge of the bed.

"Thanks Leroy!" she sang, bouncing on the firm mattress and then interlacing her fingers in front of her. This would be a nice new home, and she would have lots of people to play with.

Leroy closed the door without responding. The lock slid into place with a solid clunk, leaving Eliza alone at last.

Her thoughts went back to the strange girl in the elevator. She didn't have friends. But one day soon, she would try to make friends with that girl.

Hopping off the bed, Eliza swayed to the window, her quiet song drifting around her. The sun was just beginning to set over the tall trees in the distance, the warm southern wind blowing the tops gently. Rosy clouds graced the sky.

Looking down, Eliza saw her room overlooked a walled-in garden, dotted with green shrubs and numerous wildflowers. As the sun set and the shadows lengthened, the beautiful colors faded to black, casting the garden in darkness.

Above her, the vent purred to life and cold air drifted down.

Eliza exhaled and closed her eyes as the cool air enveloped her. An image flashed briefly; silver eyes atop a silver smile. The vision made her feel safe, protected.

Her memory continued to tumble around, trying to fill in the missing chunks. There was something she was supposed to do, some goal she'd had in mind, but she couldn't seem to recall it now. Someone was definitely out there, watching her, waiting for her. It was all a matter of time before she found them or they found her.

Eliza sighed happily and opened her eyes, waving goodnight to the dark flowers far below.

ACKNOWLEDGMENTS

Here I am, at the very end of my first book at last! I have been dreaming of this moment since 3rd grade and I would never have made it here without so many people. I would like to give Vern and Joni and the rest of the team at BHC Press a huge thank you for walking me through the publishing process and for all of their tireless support. Also, I would like to thank my amazing editor, Bailey Karfelt. Without you and your guidance this book would still be sitting on my laptop and would never have evolved to what you helped mold it to be! I would also like to thank my wonderful friend, Jill. Not only did you introduce me to BHC but you also kept me sane and made me laugh every single day. Thank you for also introducing me to Stephanie who helped me learn the ropes to become an author and was always there to give me advice and pep talks! I just have one more thank you to address and that is for my 7th and 8th grade teacher Mr. Gworek. You were the first one to acknowledge my passion for writing and tell me that I could do it. From teaching me what a lexicon was to practicing my analogies, I will always remember my time in your classroom. I hope this book will make you proud.

ABOUT THE AUTHOR

Caytlyn lives in Elmira, NY with her husband Daniel, her infant son, Jack, and her orange tabby cat, Ana who is only slightly over-weight. She can quote any Disney movie and believes that everyone should wear polka dots.

Made in the USA
Middletown, DE
15 June 2017